MIRANDA LEE

Two-Week Wife

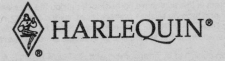

HARLEQUIN®

TORONTO • NEW YORK • LONDON
AMSTERDAM • PARIS • SYDNEY • HAMBURG
STOCKHOLM • ATHENS • TOKYO • MILAN • MADRID
PRAGUE • WARSAW • BUDAPEST • AUCKLAND

ISBN 0-373-11978-X

TWO-WEEK WIFE

First North American Publication 1998.

Copyright © 1997 by Miranda Lee.

CHAPTER ONE

'ADAM,' Bianca said in that softly persuasive voice he knew oh, so well. 'I...er...I...um...Well, I have this little problem, you see, and I'm afraid I need your help...'

Adam's stomach contracted. He turned slowly from where he'd been pouring himself a drink, the whisky decanter and glass still in his hands. He'd just walked in the door after one hell of a Saturday afternoon at Randwick races and wasn't in the mood for one of Bianca's 'little problems.'

All sorts of possibilities flittered through his mind. She'd clobbered some poor bloke who'd patted or pinched her on the bottom—Bianca had one of those bottoms men could not resist.

Or she'd given all the housekeeping money away to a good cause. *Again.*

Or... His eyes darted swiftly around the unit. God, don't tell me she's brought home some starving stray dog or cat she's found on the streets!

This she did with regular monotony, even though she knew the lease didn't allow pets in their apartment block. It always fell to him in the end to take the damned bag of bones to the RSPCA, after which Bianca would glare balefully at him for days, as though he himself had personally murdered the wretched worm-ridden animal.

Relief flooded through him when the spacious and relatively uncluttered living room showed no sign of such a stray. Besides, Bianca wouldn't be nervous about something like that, he finally realised. She would be defiant and rebellious.

And she *was* nervous. More than he could ever remember seeing her before.

His stomach tightened another notch.

Hell, he hoped she wasn't pregnant by her latest beefcake boyfriend, and wanted *him*—her schnook-head flatmate and first best friend—to pay for an abortion.

Oh God, not that. Anything but that!

'For pity's sake, Bianca,' he said, almost despairingly. 'What have you done *this* time?' Adam's normally cool grey eyes projected total frustration as he glared at the woman he'd loved and hated for the past twenty-eight years.

No, not twenty-eight, he amended bitterly in his mind. Only twenty-three. He hadn't met her till their first day at kindergarten together, when he'd been five.

He'd been blubbering in a corner of the classroom, all by himself, when this amazingly grown-up and self-assured four-year-old, with big blue eyes and a glossy black ponytail tied with a red ribbon, had put an arm around his shaking shoulders and told him not to worry. *She'd* look after him. *She* wasn't at all scared because her mummy was a scripture teacher at this school and she'd been coming here for simply ages.

This little she-devil—who had been cleverly disguised as a guardian angel back then—had even known where the toilets were, which had been of real concern to him at that moment in time.

He'd been her devoted slave from that point.

He still was.

And she knew it!

He watched wryly as she made those big blue eyes look oh, so innocent. If there was one thing Bianca should not have been able to look these days, it was innocent. But she could, and it always made him melt.

'It's nothing bad, Adam,' she said, as though butter wouldn't melt in her mouth. 'Really.'

'What about dangerous?' he muttered drily. Bianca thrived on danger of the physical kind.

As a kid she'd been a tomboy and a thrill-seeker, always having to climb the highest tree in the yard, always having to play whatever sport the boys were playing and then become the best at it. She'd been able to run faster, throw further and jump higher than any of the boys in her class.

But that had all changed when she went to high school and puberty pulled her back on the field. Talent and determination alone hadn't been able to compete with the boys once the sheer disadvantage of height, weight and size had become evident.

To Bianca's chagrin, she had stopped growing at five feet three and a half, and she was burdened for ever with a very slender fine-boned figure. Even so, she'd fought to be allowed to play with the boys' soccer team, going on to become their highest goal-scorer each season.

'You're not going to try out for the Australian male soccer team now, are you?' he asked, somewhat caustically.

Bianca was still into sport in a big way. *And* sportsmen. If there was one thing guaranteed to turn her on, it was broad shoulders and a bulging set of biceps. Brains didn't come into it. Only brawn. She liked her men tall too, which was rather ironic considering her own lack of height.

Though six feet tall himself, with a far better body than Bianca gave him credit for, Adam knew he would never fulfil the criteria necessary to capture Bianca's sexual interest. Nothing sparked when she looked at him. There was no chemistry—on her side.

Adam knew this because Bianca had told him so herself, with brutal but well-meant frankness, on the night she'd turned twenty-one and he'd wasted two dozen long-stemmed red roses in trying to woo her one last time. When he'd confessed he was crazy about her, she'd declared she loved him to death, but that it was the love a girl felt for a big brother or a best friend. She was sorry, but if he couldn't accept that, then perhaps it would be better if he stayed out of her life.

She'd been right, of course. It would have been better if he'd stayed out of her life.

But he hadn't. He just couldn't. He remained her best friend, lending a fairly broad shoulder for her to cry on occasionally, and money when she was desperate enough to ask; Bianca had been brought up by her Scottish mother to 'neither a borrower, nor a lender be'.

'Don't be silly.' She pouted at him. She had pouting lips to go with that equally pouting bottom. 'I don't do things like that any more. I know I'm far too small to play with the really big boys.'

Only on the soccer field, he thought testily. It didn't stop her playing with the really big boys in the bedroom. And the bigger the better, from what he could gather.

'I wouldn't put anything past you, Bianca,' he ground out as he slopped some much needed whisky into his glass.

'You make me sound so . . . so . . .'

'Crazy?' he suggested bitingly. 'Irresponsible? Impulsive?' She was all of those things. Not to mention warm, wacky, wild and wonderful, he added to himself on a silent groan.

Lifting the glass to his lips, he downed a good gulp of straight Johnny Walker. It burnt a fiery path down his throat and into his knotted stomach.

Bianca's beautiful lips pursed further, her blue eyes narrowing, giving her an exotic, oriental look. This was enhanced by her high cheekbones, and the way her long black hair was pulled back tightly from her face. Adam had often fantasised about her being his own private geisha girl, especially when she wore the colourful red and white flowered kimono dressing-gown he'd given her last Christmas.

Bloody stupid fantasy, he thought ruefully. Bianca was as far removed from a geisha girl as any female could get!

'Just because you don't know how to have fun, Adam,' she tossed at him with haughty disdain.

He snorted and strode across the sable-coloured carpet, flopping down into his favourite brown leather armchair. 'Is that what you think you're doing when you keep changing direction in your life at the drop of a hat?' he threw up at her. 'Was it fun you were having when you came to me last year, stony broke and without a roof over your head? Was it fun earlier this year, after that loser of a boyfriend dumped you? Do you really find it fun having others pick up your pieces?'

'I do not expect you or anyone else to pick up my pieces,' she huffed and puffed. 'And I'll have you know that *I'm* the one who usually dumps my "losers of boyfriends," not the other way around.'

'At least we agree on one thing,' he said drily. 'They've all been bums so far.'

'Maybe,' she countered blithely. 'But they all had very nice bums, those bums.'

'You'd know, I suppose.' He quaffed back half the whisky, congratulating himself on the offhandedness of his reply—especially when the image of his Bianca being intimate with any part of another man's anatomy nearly killed him. 'But we have digressed. Back to your present little problem. Out with it, Bianca. I'm not in the mood for any of your female manoeuvrings tonight.'

'All right, then, you meanie. I was just trying to tell you nicely, to make you understand that I had no idea this would eventuate. When the situation first arose, I didn't *have* to involve you personally at all, but something unexpected has happened and now I have no alternative.'

Adam didn't have a clue as to what she was talking about. But he feared he would. Soon. Only too well.

Bianca sat down on the sofa-end nearest his chair and leant towards him with the most heart-warmingly pleading look on her lovely face. 'Please don't be mad at me, Adam,' she said, in a voice which would have melted concrete.

For a split second Adam felt himself begin to go to mush, before cold, hard reality had him getting a firm handle on his ongoing weakness for this incorrigible creature. She was going to use him again, as she had used him for years.

No more, he vowed staunchly. No more!

'Out with it, Bianca,' he snapped. 'No more bull. Just give me the facts, and *I'll* decide if I'm going to be involved or not.'

Her startled eyes betrayed surprise at his hard stance. She straightened her spine, then rocked her shoulders slightly from side to side in the characteristic gesture which usually preceded defiance or outright rebellion. Her chin shot up. Her eyes flashed and her mouth tightened. 'There's no need to take that tone.'

'I'll best be the judge of that, thank you. Now just spit it out, woman!'

'Very well. It's to do with my mother.'

'What about your mother?' Adam frowned. Bianca's mum was a widow and had gone back to Scotland to live several years before. She'd been very lonely after her husband had been killed in a drag-racing accident.

Bianca was her only child and not much company once she'd finished university and had started flitting round the world on never-ending backpacking holidays. She only returned long enough to pick up a few months' work, thereby saving up enough to be off again.

Mrs Peterson had several brothers and sisters back in Scotland, so it had made sense for her to return to her homeland. Then, six months ago in May, she'd been diagnosed with breast cancer.

'Is she worse?' he asked worriedly. 'Do you need some more money to go and see her again?'

'No to both those questions. Which is just as well. I haven't finished paying you back for the last ticket to Edinburgh you bought me.'

True, he thought ruefully. Which was the only reason she'd stayed in one job and one place for so long. No doubt as soon as her debt was paid she'd be off again on some new adventure, trekking through the Himalayas or skiing down the mountain slopes of St Moritz.

'No, Mum's much better,' Bianca was saying. 'And there's every chance that the cancer won't come back.'

'Then what's the problem? I don't understand.'

'She's coming out here for a fortnight's visit, that's what. Her plane touches down next Saturday afternoon—a week from today. Her brothers and sisters all pitched in and bought her a return flight to Sydney.'

'Well, what's the problem in that? You should be thrilled. Oh, I see . . . you want her to stay here. That's no trouble, Bianca. I don't mind. I'm hardly here these days anyway, and there are two beds in your room, aren't there?'

'That's the problem,' she muttered.

Adam blinked his confusion. 'The beds in your room are a problem?'

'Yes.'

'Why?'

'Because Mum won't be expecting me to occupy one, that's why.'

'You've lost me, Bianca.'

Her sigh was expressive. 'It's like this, Adam. Mum thinks we're married. Naturally she'll be expecting me to be sleeping in *your* bed. And she'll also expect you to be around a bit more than you have been lately. God knows what you've been up to. If I didn't know better I'd think you were avoiding me.'

'She . . . thinks . . . we're . . . married,' he repeated slowly, his eyes narrowing with each word.

'Don't look at me like that, Adam. I didn't mean any harm. Honestly. But when I was over there in May she looked so darned ill. Try to understand...I thought she was going to die!

'I knew she'd always wanted to see me settled—preferably with you—so I told her what would make her happy. I said we were engaged and going to be married. Then after I came back and she kept hanging in there I had no alternative but to follow through. So I sent her some selective photos from Michelle's wedding and said it was ours.'

Adam was shaking his head in utter disbelief. 'How, in God's name, did you pull *that* off? You weren't even wearing *white* that day!'

'My bridesmaid dress was pale pink and could easily pass for a wedding dress. Besides, Mum wouldn't have expected me to have a traditional wedding with a big white dress. And you looked suitably bridegroomy in your best man outfit.

'Luckily with it being your sister's wedding, all your family were there. And on top of that, we had a lot of shots taken together, being partners for the day. Mum thought you looked very handsome, by the way. Oh, and remember those queen-sized sheets she sent, and which I gave you for your bed? They...er....they were our wedding present.'

Adam's hand clenched tightly around the glass he was holding. Fury that she would perpetrate this fiasco without even consulting him had his blood bubbling with heated anger along his veins. Naturally she hadn't expected to get caught. She'd probably thought her poor mum would safely pass away before her outrageous lies came to light.

That was always the way with Bianca. She never thought things through to all their possible eventualities and consequences. She always just plunged into some mad caper or other, without worrying or working out how it might affect others.

Never had this been more evident than on the occasion she'd come to him at the age of seventeen and asked him to relieve her of her virginity. Not for reasons of romance, mind. Simply out of curiosity. And she was tired, she'd said, of being the only girl in her group who hadn't done it. Tired of having to defend her lack of male admirers.

Back then, boys hadn't gone for Bianca all that much. Of course, *she'd* always thought it was because of her lack of boobs, but that hadn't been so at all. It had simply been because they were used to treating her like a mate, not an object of male desire.

He'd been the only boy in school who'd fancied her like mad. And she'd known it. What she *hadn't* known, when she'd asked this favour of him, was that he'd been a virgin too, back then. A bit of an embarrassment, really, being a male virgin at eighteen. His mates had used to rag him about it all the time.

He cringed now to think of the total mess he'd made of 'relieving' Bianca of her virginity—and himself of his own. He'd been so bloody nervous. Terrified, in fact. He'd been scared of hurting her, scared of coming too soon, scared of not being able to get the damned condom on properly.

The act itself had turned into an absolute disaster, with most of his fears coming to pass. In the end, he *had* hurt her, *and* it had all been over too soon. As for the damned condom...he had no idea how that had eventually assumed its rightful position. No doubt more by accident than design.

What should have been the most marvellous moment of his life had deteriorated into being the most embarrassing and definitely the most humiliating.

He could still recall the various expressions on her face during the ten-second event. Pain had been followed by a few moments of frowning frustration, culminating in something even worse... relief when the act had come to a very rapid conclusion, obviously without her experiencing one single moment of pleasure, let alone satisfaction.

Afterwards she'd been uncharacteristically silent, and he'd skulked off home feeling utterly crushed and totally deflated.

The only good to come out of that night had been that the experience had seemed to turn Bianca off sex for the next few years. She'd probably concluded it wasn't worth bothering about, till a super-macho martial arts instructor, whose class she'd enrolled in during her last year at uni, had taken her uninterest in him as the ultimate challenge and then proceeded to show her that sex was nothing like what she'd experienced that night. He'd apparently been a fantastic lover, with a body any girl would drool over and a technique to match.

From that moment she'd been hooked—not only on the pleasures of the flesh, but on that sort of male. After Mr Black Belt, she was programmed to believe that arousal and satisfaction were synonymous with an ultra-fit, muscle-bound body and a super-stud mentality.

Adam had always wanted the opportunity to show Bianca he was no longer the sexual klutz he'd been at eighteen, but she would never give him that opportunity. Her mind was fixed against him, her preconceptions set in concrete. He'd thought he'd come to terms with this, but now he realised he hadn't. Not for a moment.

He wanted her now more than ever, and could not bear the thought of spending a single second in the same bed as her without being able to touch her.

Which was what she would surely ask of him if he agreed to go along with this masquerade of a marriage. She would expect him to allow her to climb into his bed every night for the duration of her mother's stay. And she would also expect him not to lay a single hand on her.

Such a prospect was beyond the pale. He would not do it. He was a man, not a mouse, and it was high time Bianca recognised that fact.

Uncurling his white-knuckled fingers, he placed the empty glass down on a side-table and stood up.

CHAPTER TWO

'WHAT do you mean ... *no*?' she shouted after him as he disappeared down the hallway.

'I mean *no*!' he called back over his shoulder. 'I won't go along with it. You married us, Bianca. Now you'll just have to divorce us.'

Bianca gaped after him for a moment before snapping her mouth shut. Exasperation mixed with irritation as she rolled her eyes. She'd had a feeling he was going to be difficult about this. And she'd damned well been right!

Underneath, however, she still felt confident she could bring him round. Michelle always said she could twist Adam around her little finger. Bianca wasn't fond of that phrase, but she could not deny there was some truth in it. Just as there was some truth in Michelle's belief that her brother was still in love with his old schoolfriend.

Bianca sometimes felt guilty about taking advantage of Adam's lingering and largely unrequited passion for her. She'd shamelessly used his affection for her in the past. She supposed she was still doing it to a degree.

Though, to be fair to herself, she'd warned him never to hope things would change. She loved him to death but she did not desire him. It was as simple as that.

Actually, now that she thought about it, she wasn't so sure Adam *was* in love with her any more. There'd been a steady stream of girlfriends paraded through this place since she'd come to live here a year ago—all blonde bimbo types, with legs that went up to their armpits and busts which made Bianca go green with envy. If he was pining after *her*, then he was making a darned good fist of hiding it.

This realisation piqued her somewhat. She'd become used to the notion that Adam was still in love with her. It had become a secret balm to soothe her battered ego on occasions, to reassure her that she was worthy of being loved, that there was more to her than being just the flighty piece of goods several men had called her.

Bianca frowned dissatisfaction at this train of thought. It seemed she just wasn't ready yet to give up Adam's status as her secret admirer. Knowing he was always there for her was the one steadying factor in her life—he was a rock she could rely on when all else failed.

A type of panic began to set in. She could not bear the thought that he might one day cut her out of his life. For ever. She'd be lost without him. Yet if he wasn't in love with her any more, then it was bound to happen one day...

Maybe he isn't still madly in love with me, she amended in desperation. But he *does* care about me.

Just as she cared about him. Deeply. He'd touched something in her from that first day at kindergarten, when she'd spied him in a corner crying his heart out. All during their school days she'd felt compelled to look after him, for he'd been such a sweetie. And such a hopeless nerd of a boy!

Around sixteen, he'd shot up suddenly—all gangly legs, long, greasy hair and pimples. Talk about unattractive! By their last year at school he'd improved somewhat in looks, but by then he'd become shy and awkward around girls. One day she'd overheard several of his so-called mates taunting him over his lack of success with the opposite sex. They'd called him cruel names and made him look small.

Bianca had felt sorry for him, *so* sorry that she'd decided to sacrifice her own virginity for the sake of his. It was the least she could do, she'd felt, for her very best friend.

Oddly enough, she still could not think of that night without being besieged by the most confused feelings. He'd been absolutely hopeless at it. And it had hurt like hell. Yet, for all that, she'd been unbearably moved by the experience—had had to battle hard not to cry afterwards. There had been something so incredibly sweet about his appalling nerves, not to mention the look on his face.

Bianca tried to blot out the disturbing memory as she launched herself up from the sofa and raced after Adam down the hallway.

Of course there'd been something incredibly sweet about it, she dismissed with irritable impatience. Adam was an incredibly sweet person. Thank God. And as such, he could not keep saying no to her once she pointed out how much the truth would distress her mother. He liked her mother, almost as much as her mother liked him.

Bianca made it into his bedroom just in time to see him slam the *en suite* bathroom's door shut. She heard the lock snap into place, followed by the sound of the shower being turned on full.

Pummelling on the door didn't seem like a good idea, so she decided to wait patiently for his return. Meanwhile she picked up the clothes he'd strewn around the room in his anger.

Bianca shook her head in disbelief as she hung up his shirt and trousers. Messiness was as unlike him as his outburst of anger. The adult Adam was a quiet, coolly controlled individual—a highly intelligent but rather reserved man who liked order and tidiness. He was a maths lecturer at Sydney University, and his chief hobby was working out mathematically based systems for winning money at the races.

With some success apparently, since he was now driving a new BMW. His salary alone would not have provided that, and his family had no more money than hers.

She was tucking a sock into each shoe when the bathroom door was wrenched open. A cloud of steam emerged first, through which strode Adam, swathed from neck to ankle in his favourite red towelling robe which was as huge as it was thick.

Amazingly cold grey eyes settled on her as he sashed it tightly around his waist. 'That won't work either,' he said brusquely.

'What?'

'Picking up after me. Sweet-talking's a waste of time too. You've overstepped the mark, Bianca, and I'm not going to save your butt this time. Your mother will probably live for donkey's years and I'm not going to be permanently saddled with the ridiculous role of pretending to be your long-suffering husband.'

'R-ridiculous!' she spluttered. 'Long-*suffering*?'

A coating of dry amusement brought a gleam to his steely gaze. 'You don't honestly think any sane man would want to be your *real* husband, do you? Only a fool or a masochist would volunteer for *that* job.'

Bianca blinked her shock. This was her sweet Adam talking to her like this? And looking at her like that?

'You look surprised, darling,' he went on with chilling indifference as he casually raked his hands through his wet dark hair. 'Don't tell me you've believed all that rubbish my sister's been feeding you all these years about my still being in love with you?'

Bianca's mouth fell inelegantly open. Adam's laugh scraped down her spine like chalk on a blackboard.

'Michelle's such a romantic,' he said, his voice as cynically amused as his eyes. 'I admit I had the most awful crush on you all through school. I even clung to my warped passion through our university days. But I finally outgrew it—for which I have you to thank, Bianca.

'You really made me see the truth that night you turned twenty-one. I was wasting my time wanting you. So I turned my futile fantasies from fiction to fact with another female later that evening, and frankly I haven't looked back since.'

Bianca was stung to the quick by his words. *And* by the images they evoked. 'You mean I wasted my guilt on you that night?' she burst out angrily. 'There I was, thinking I'd broken your heart, when in truth you were off...you were off...' She huffed and puffed to stop herself saying the crudity which had sprung onto the tip of her tongue.

'I was off making some other more grateful girl happy?' he suggested sarcastically.

'Who was it?' she demanded to know, her mind racing along with her heart. 'Not that awful Tracy. My God, she'd sleep with anyone, that trollop!'

'Thank you for the compliment, darling. But, no, it wasn't Tracy. It was Laura.'

Laura!

Bianca was speechless. Laura had not been one of their group. She'd been a friend of a friend of a friend, who'd somehow been at her party by accident. Thirty if she was a day, but an absolutely stunning blonde with an absolutely stunning figure.

'I don't believe you!' she choked out, hurt beyond belief by this almost ancient betrayal of his so-called love for her.

'Don't you? Poor Bianca.' His smile was not at all sweet. 'Has someone stolen your lollipop, darling? Won't naughty Adam play the game any more?'

Her mouth returned to its earlier goldfish imitation.

Adam reached out and flicked her chin upwards, so her teeth snapped together. His eyes were narrowed and cruel-looking. He was nothing at all like the Adam she knew and loved.

'I suggest you toddle off now, sweetheart, and make up a new story to tell your mother. I'm sure you can come up with one, being such an inventive and imaginative little minx. If you're really stuck, you could always try the truth!'

Bianca's startled tongue-tiedness didn't last for long, and was quickly replaced by indignant and sceptical outrage. 'I don't believe any of this! Have you been drinking? Did you lose all your money at the races? This isn't like you at all, Adam.'

He gripped her shoulders and pushed her down into a sitting position on the end of the bed. 'Yes, I've been drinking,' he agreed in a steely tone. 'And, yes, I did lose a good deal at the races today, which didn't please me at all. But you're quite wrong when you think this isn't like me. It is. It's the new me.'

'The new you?' she repeated blankly.

'I've been too soft with you for too long, Bianca. It's done your character no good. No good at all. You think you can do as you please where I'm concerned. You think you can run rings around me. Well, you can't anymore, sweetness. I'm awake to you now. Actually, I have been for ages, but it didn't suit me to make a stand. It does now.'

'Why now?' she threw back up at him, feeling suddenly angry. How dared he let her think he loved her all this time when he didn't?

'Because I've met someone,' he said. 'Someone I intend asking to marry me. Hard to do that when I'm pretending to be married to someone else, don't you think?'

Bianca felt her world go slightly out of kilter for a moment. Adam had fallen in love? He was going to get married?

Her heart squeezed tight. Her stomach flipped over. 'I don't believe you!'

He straightened, laughing. 'You do seem to be having trouble with believing me today. Tell me what you don't believe.'

She levered herself to her feet, shaken to find that her legs felt like jelly. 'I don't believe you've met someone. You haven't brought a girl home here once this last month. You're just making her up.'

But at the back of her mind Bianca was remembering all those nights Adam hadn't come home lately. She'd presumed he was sleeping over in his room at the university, which he sometimes did. Now she saw there could be a very different explanation for his many absences.

He laughed again. 'You're really grasping at straws, you know that? The reason I didn't bring Sophie here was because I wanted our relationship to last. What chance did I have with any of my other girlfriends after they'd met *you* as my flatmate?

'They always took one look at you and were instantly jealous and suspicious. Nothing I could ever say would convince them our friendship was purely platonic. They were all convinced we were secret lovers. An impression you deliberately seemed to foster, I might add.'

'I did not!' she denied hotly. But underneath she knew she had. She'd never felt any of those bimbos were good enough for Adam. She'd only been protecting him by getting rid of them.

'You never wanted me, Bianca,' he swept on, a cold rage settling into his eyes. 'But you didn't want anyone else to have me either. You've been a very greedy little girl. And very selfish. It's time you stopped thinking of no one but yourself.'

'But that's not true,' she wailed, hating this new Adam and the way he was making her feel. 'I was thinking of my mother when I told her...what I told her.' Tears filled her eyes, tears of temper more than distress. 'You have no right to say these rotten things to me. You're being so hateful!'

'The truth often hurts.'

The truth, she thought savagely. The truth was that *her* Adam was going to marry someone else! Just the thought of it was like a dagger in her heart. God knows why. She didn't want to marry him herself. She didn't want to marry *any* man.

Marriage, in Bianca's opinion, would be a living death for someone like her. She was just like her father in that respect, craving change and excitement all the time. She didn't like the idea of settling down and having children any more than he had.

Her dad had married in the throes of a whirlwind passion, then spent the next twenty years finding satisfaction outside of the marital bed. Bianca suspected she might be just as fickle. There hadn't been a male yet to hold her sexual interest beyond six months. She suspected none ever would.

'So who is this Sophie you're going to marry?' she demanded to know.

'Oh, no, you don't,' Adam retorted with a dry chuckle. 'I'm going to keep her well away from you, Madam Mischief-Maker.'

'Where do you sleep with her?'

'None of your business. Do I ask you where you copulate with your latest boyfriend?'

'You can, if you like. But Derek and I have parted company. He was beginning to bore me.'

'Gee whiz, what happened? Didn't you fall asleep straight afterwards one night? Were you actually forced to make conversation with Mr Macho-Man?'

Bianca could feel a smile begin to tug at her lips. It was a good description for Derek, who was a professional weight-lifter with more muscles than mental capacity. 'Something like that,' she said.

Their eyes met, and that old camaraderie which had sustained their friendship all these years struggled to the surface. She'd always been able to tell Adam pretty much anything. And she'd never been able to shock him. He'd always listened and always given her sound advice, but never condemned. He was still her best friend, she realised, her heart squeezing tight as a wry smile began to play around his mouth.

Instinctively she reached out to place an intimate hand on his arm. 'Sophie doesn't have to know, Adam,' she said pleadingly. 'Mum will soon be gone, back to Scotland. Please ... I don't want to spoil her trip by telling her the truth just yet. I promise I'll write to her after she's gone back and make up something to get you permanently off the hook.'

She held her breath as he simply stared at her.

Please say yes, she was silently willing him. Please ...

His sigh was weary as he removed her hand from his arm. 'You never know when to give up, do you? Now let me make this quite clear. I am not going to play happy husband for you and your mother. I am not going to let you sleep in my bed while she's here, unless I'm not in it. I am not going to be at your beck and call, or dance to any tune you might choose to play.'

Bianca's dismay was only exceeded by her panic. 'But whatever am I going to tell her?'

'Tell her whatever story you fancy, Bianca, only make it convincing. You have a choice: either telling the truth, or inventing a temporary separation or impending divorce. Believe me when I tell you I have somewhere I can lay my head for the duration of that fortnight, so you don't have to worry your pretty little head about where I'll sleep.'

Bianca glared at him while he shepherded her out of his bedroom. 'Now, if you don't mind, I'd like to get dressed. I'm going out.' And he firmly closed and locked his door.

CHAPTER THREE

ADAM closed his eyes as he leant against the door.

God damn Bianca for making him lie like that!

He had no intention of asking Sophie to marry him. Hell, he'd only just met the girl the previous week.

He also hadn't been going to go out tonight. He was tired after his unsuccessful foray at the races. He would have liked nothing better than to settle down in front of the TV with his feet up and have Bianca dish him up one of her interesting meals.

She was a fantastic cook, and spoiled him whenever he was at home in that regard. It was one of the plusses among the many negatives in having her around.

But he'd be blowed if he'd stay at home tonight now! He'd have to sleep over at the penthouse, he supposed, even though it would still smell of paint. He didn't have a date with Sophie, as Bianca would undoubtedly conclude. But he wished he had.

A night in bed with Sophie would blot Bianca out of his mind for a few hours at least. Sophie was everything Bianca wasn't. Tall and curvy, with long blonde hair, wide hips and breasts like melons. He'd learnt from Laura many years ago never to date a girl who reminded him in any way of the

31

heartless creature who'd told him she felt nothing
when she looked at him. Generally he confined
himself to bedding busty blondes, with the oc-
casional redhead thrown in for variety. Brunettes
never stood a chance.

Sophie was a minor actress, sleeping her way up
in the world with gay abandon. He'd met her last
Saturday night at the new Darling Harbour Casino,
where she was working as a croupier between bit
roles in movies. No doubt she'd thought he was a
real high-roller, laying thousand-dollar bets. Which
he was, he supposed.

Gambling had always paid off for Adam, because he approached it with a cool head and math-
ematical skill. Bianca would be stunned at how
much money it had brought him over the years...if
he ever chose to tell her. She thought he confined
his gambling to the races. She also thought he lost
more than he won.

Racing was all very well, in small doses, but the
really big money was to be made in the casinos.
Unfortunately, he had to keep changing venues,
because management soon spotted professional
gamblers, and had a dim view of clients capable of
counting cards or who used other systems which
could regularly beat the house.

Bianca had no idea of his weekend trips inter-
state, to the casinos in Melbourne, Hobart,
Adelaide and even Perth, nor of the elegant,
sophisticated and very accommodating women who
threw themselves at him on those occasions. It

stroked his ego to note that they had no trouble with 'spark' when they looked at him, as Bianca did. Hell, they fairly went up in flames when he touched them.

Fortunately, the opening of a new casino in Sydney had brought him a much closer venue—for gambling and otherwise. The night he'd met Sophie, he'd been trying one of his newer systems on the blackjack table, though his concentration had been shot to pieces. He'd been thinking about Bianca spending the weekend up the coast at some sleazy motel with darling Derek. She hadn't been bored with him seven days ago. Far from it!

Sophie had given him the eye as she'd dealt him the cards, so his bruised ego had taken her home to her place after she finished up. He hadn't given Bianca a single thought till he'd woken the next morning to brown eyes instead of blue, and blonde hair instead of black.

Swearing at the memory, Adam levered himself away from the door, throwing off his robe as he strode over to his built-in wardrobe.

He began to agonise, as he dragged on some clothes, about whether he'd ever marry.

Probably not, came the savagely rueful acceptance. He'd only ever wanted one girl as his wife and the mother of his children. How could he settle for second-best?

No, he'd be having one-night stands with blonde bimbos when he was eighty—paid for, by then—

and dreaming of what might have been, if only he
hadn't been such a useless schmuck at eighteen!

He glanced down at the old jeans he'd automatically pulled on and thought of all the swanky
clothes he'd recently installed in the penthouse instead of the boot of his car—the ones he wore in
his secret life as gambler and lover extraordinaire.
The Italian suits. The tuxedos. The black silk
pyjamas and dressing gowns.

He shook his head at himself, for he knew that
that life wasn't real. It would one day come to an
end. It was a game. Thankfully a prosperous game,
while his wits and courage were up to it, but still
essentially a game—to be played as a boost to his
ego and bank balance as well as a much needed
diversion from the distress real life kept bringing
him.

Real life was outside this door, waiting for him,
waiting to try to change his mind about being her
pretend husband.

He would have to be strong. Already he was
feeling guilty. Already he was weakening. Tempting
thoughts began infiltrating his brain. Maybe he
would enjoy the pretence? Maybe he could lie there
at night beside her and fantasise? Maybe she'd be
so grateful to him that she'd let him...?

His teeth clenched down hard in his jaw. He
didn't want her bloody gratitude. He wanted what
she willingly gave those other guys. He wanted her
passion and her desire. He wanted her sexy little

body, naked and panting beneath him, begging him to go on, desperate for him...

Adam swore as he became hotly aware that his fantasy had swiftly transferred to a hard, aching reality. He dragged a sloppy Joe down over his thudding heart and vowed not to weaken one iota.

Even if she got down on her hands and knees before him, he would not budge an inch.

A darkly ironic smile creased his mouth as he shoved his feet into battered trainers.

Let's not go too far, Adam, came the wicked thought. Bianca on her hands and knees was a perverse and powerfully persuasive prospect. Too bad it would never come about. He would give anything to have her at his mercy. Anything!

Bianca spun round from the kitchen sink when she heard Adam's bedroom door bang. Oh, dear. He still sounded very angry. What to do? How best to approach him?

Appeal to his sense of compassion, she decided, and raced out to head him off before he could leave. The sight of him dressed in old clothes distracted her for a second.

'Oh!' she exclaimed. 'So you're not taking the soon-to-be fiancée out tonight?' she asked tartly, and immediately bit her bottom lip. Wrong tack, you fool.

'We're staying in,' he drawled. 'Watching videos and searching for the meaning of life.'

Bianca was taken aback by his sarcasm. He really was in a filthy mood. Perhaps she should leave appealing to his compassion till tomorrow.

But what if he didn't come home tomorrow? He was staying away from the flat more and more these days—obviously at this Sophie's place.

'Adam, when can we talk about this further?' she asked, in her most apologetic and reasonable tone. 'I know you're angry with me, and I'm sorry. I should have told you before this.'

'You shouldn't have done it at all!'

'Yes, you're right. I'm sorry.'

'Bianca, saying sorry is not always enough.'

Bianca could feel mutiny brewing inside her heart. Why was he being so damned difficult about this? Was she asking so much? Two miserable weeks of pretending to be her husband and then he was off the hook to marry this . . . this Sophie creature.

'You always said I could count on you,' she pointed out rather sulkily.

'You can. In things that count.'

She pouted her displeasure. 'I would do it for you.'

'Do what?'

'Pretend to be your wife.'

'Really? That's an interesting thought. But I don't need a pretend wife. I'm going to have a real one.'

Bianca still hadn't come to terms with that. Still, there was a many a slip twixt the engagement and the altar. If this Sophie was anything like his previous girlfriends he'd soon be bored to death with her. None of those bimbos had had enough brains to boil water.

'So what do you expect me to tell Mum?' she asked defiantly.

He shrugged. 'That's your problem.'

'I'm not going to tell her I lied, Adam.'

'Heaven forbid. Tell you what, though. I'll stay away the whole fortnight. You tell your mum we're having a trial separation. Then, later, you can write and say that it didn't work out and we're divorced.'

'She'll be very upset.'

'Only if you are. Tell her that it was an amicable parting and that we're still good friends. That's the best I can do.'

Bianca pressed her lips tightly together to stop herself from saying what she thought of him and his so-called friendship. When the chips were down, it had proved about as strong as his so-called love! 'Is that your final word on the matter?'

'It is.'

'Then to hell with you, Adam Marsden. You're not the man I thought you were. As soon as Mum goes home to Scotland, I'll be finding somewhere else to live.'

His sudden stillness raised one last grain of hope in her breast. She could have sworn regret flashed momentarily in his eyes. But then they cooled perceptively and her heart sank.

'I think that would be best for all concerned, Bianca,' he said, with casual indifference.

All of a sudden she wanted to cry. Or to scream. Or both. Instead, she gave him an icy glare. 'I will never ask you for another thing. Not as long as I live. I will have trouble even speaking to you!'

His face hardened. 'Good.'

'I had no idea you were such a bastard! To think I once believed you loved me!'

The cruellest little smile pulled at his mouth. 'The things we have to live with,' came his sarcastic remark.

Bianca could only stare at him. 'I don't know you at all, do I? You've become a stranger!'

'A stranger?' he repeated idly. 'Yes, you could be right.'

And, with that devil's smile still playing on his lips, he picked up his car keys from where he always left them in the ashtray on the coffee-table and walked out on her.

CHAPTER FOUR

BIANCA was as good as her word. She didn't ask Adam for another thing all week. Neither did she speak to him.

Hard to, when he wasn't there.

He'd come back briefly on the Sunday evening, collected some clothes, told her curtly he'd be staying elsewhere for the following three weeks and departed again.

It turned out to be the loneliest, most wretched week Bianca had ever spent in her life. She missed Adam terribly. OK, so they hadn't been living in each other's pockets lately, but he was usually there a few nights a week, and always on a Sunday afternoon. She liked having him around to talk to and cook for. He gave her life purpose, especially now she'd given Derek the flick.

Truly, she didn't know what she'd ever seen in that big lug. He had a great body to look at and touch, but this time—amazingly—she'd wanted more. She'd wanted a boyfriend with brains as well as brawn.

Adam had been so right about dear Derek's lack of grey matter. This had come home to her during their drive up to Foster last Saturday. Four hours had never seemed so long. She'd been bored to tears before they'd even arrived at the beachside town.

Derek had not been pleased when she'd told him she wanted separate rooms. She hadn't actually been to bed with him as yet, and he'd no doubt been expecting a real orgy that weekend. Still, it hadn't been long before he'd started talking about some other girl he'd met down at the gym that week. Clearly, his girlfriends were just interchangeable sex objects.

A bit like *your* boyfriends, darling, came that horrid voice which had seemed to keep popping into her head ever since her fight with Adam. It told her all sorts of things she didn't want to hear about herself. Like how shallow she was. And how selfish.

Which she obviously was! Otherwise she would have been happy that Adam had fallen in love and was going to get married. Instead, she resented the thought. She certainly resented this Sophie. More than resented her. She hated her. And she didn't even know the girl.

Depression began to set in as each day dragged by. November was a fairly slow month in the section of the accountancy firm where she was currently employed. Her job description as 'taxation consultant' sounded far grander than the actual work she did—giving tax advice to clients and preparing their tax returns.

She'd have to find herself a new job soon. This one paid well, but it was as boring as anything. She'd only stuck at it because she owed Adam money. There were far too many moments during each day when her mind was not occupied, and then she would begin thinking of what she was going to tell her mother about her supposed marriage to Adam.

Night-times were worse. It took her ages to fall asleep, her thoughts going round and round. She started taking extra aerobics classes at the gym every evening, working herself so hard she should have slept like a log every night.

Instead, she tossed and turned, guilt warring with irritation.

Irritation was definitely winning by Wednesday night.

If only Adam had been co-operative, she started thinking furiously. If only he hadn't fallen in love with that stupid Sophie. If only he was still in love with *me*!

By Thursday night her conscience took over again. She was being shallow and selfish, thinking of no one but herself. She should never have lied to her mother in the first place. Lying was never a good idea. Honesty was indeed the best policy.

By the time she fell asleep on the Thursday night, Bianca had decided to ring Adam at the university the next morning, beg his forgiveness and promise to tell her mother the truth if only he'd come home to live.

Friday dawned to the sound of the telephone ringing in the flat, and she jumped out of bed, certain it was Adam. After all, a friendship such as theirs could not be destroyed so easily. He was probably feeling as guilty as she was, she thought as she raced to answer, her heart pounding as she snatched up the receiver.

'Hello? Is that you, Adam?' Even as she said the words she knew she was wrong. For the beeps on the line told her this was a long-distance call.

''Fraid not, lass,' a male voice said, with a Scottish accent. 'If that's Bianca, this is your Uncle Stewart.'

'Uncle Stewart?' Her heart squeezed tight. Something had gone wrong with her mother. She wasn't coming. She was dying!

All the blood drained from her face and she slumped against the telephone table. 'Oh, God,' she groaned. 'What's happened?'

'Now don't jump to conclusions, lass. Your mother's fine. She's just taken an earlier flight. It arrives around five this afternoon, not on Saturday. Is that OK? Can you meet it?'

'Yes, of course!' Bianca exclaimed, relief making her feel better than she had all week. 'But why did she do that?'

'A friend was able to upgrade her to business class on that flight for no extra money, so it seemed silly not to take it.'

'I'll say.'

'I won't keep you, lass. This is costing me a fortune. Look after your mother.'

'I will, Uncle Stewart. And thanks so much for helping with her fare.'

'No trouble. She deserves it. Bye for now.'
'Bye.'

Bianca hung up, feeling excited yet slightly sick. Her mother's imminent arrival brought home to her the fact that there was one thing less advisable than lying to her mum, and that was owning up to lying to her.

Bianca knew then that she just couldn't do it. She was going to stick to her marriage story, which meant it was better if Adam stayed right away. So there would be no phone call to the university, no begging for forgiveness. She would just have to make up some plausible story to explain Adam's absence.

Perhaps she could say the university had sent him on an unexpected mission to deepest, darkest Africa, to teach calculus to underprivileged pygmies!

Five-fifteen that afternoon found Bianca parking her car in the international terminal car park, feeling more than a little flustered. She'd had no trouble getting time off from work, but her old rusted-out heap of a car had decided not to start after sitting in the hot November sun all day, and she'd had to ring the Road Service Company to come and get it going.

Luckily, the problem had only been dirty points, and she was soon on her way. But time had been lost, peak hour had arrived and it had taken her much longer to get from the office in Crows Nest through the harbour tunnel and out to busy Mascot.

Her watch said twenty past five by the time she made it inside the blessedly air-conditioned terminal building.

A check of the overhead screens showed the flight had landed pretty well on time, ten minutes earlier. Bianca hurried along to Gate B, still feeling hot and bothered, and very grateful that it would be a while before her mother got through Customs.

A quick trip to the Ladies' revived her melting make-up and limp hair, which she secured high on her head in a shiny blue scrunchie. Her mother always complained she never made the most of her looks, so she'd made a special effort to look pretty today, wearing one of the few feminine outfits she owned—a flowing skirt and matching blouse in a flowery print of blues and mauves.

Bianca gnawed at her bottom lip as she washed her hands, hoping the old friendship ring Adam had given her once long ago would pass as a wedding ring. She was not the owner of much jewellery, and it was the best she could rustle up at the last minute. At least it was fairly plain and made of gold.

Taking a deep, gathering breath, Bianca smiled at herself in the mirror and told herself to be natural, or her mother would know something was up. May Peterson had a nose for lies, and liars.

Bianca was shocked on her return to Gate B to see her mother already there, frowning as she looked around the milling crowd for a familiar face. It seemed business class passengers were shunted through Customs a darned sight faster than the economy section in which Bianca usually travelled.

Mrs Peterson spotted her daughter and tears swiftly replaced the worry in her eyes. Bianca felt her own eyes flood as she hurried forward and threw her arms around the only person in the world who truly loved and understood her.

Till this week, she'd thought Adam did as well. But she'd been wrong about that. The thought hurt her more than she liked to admit, even to herself.

The hug was long and touchingly silent. The two women embraced tightly, no words necessary. Or perhaps neither was capable of speaking for a few moments. Finally, Bianca drew back to look her mother over.

'God, you look good!' she exclaimed.

And she did. Nothing at all like the frail, wan woman who'd been lying in that hospital bed last May. There was flesh on her bones, colour in her face and that old sparkle in her pretty blue eyes. For a woman of fifty who'd been battling cancer all year, she looked bloody marvellous!

Bianca stood there, a silly grin on her face as she thanked God for the miracle He'd obviously performed in answer to her many prayers. Yet, down deep in her heart, she still feared that the battle was not yet over, the fight not yet completely won. As such, she was not going to say or do anything to cause her mother extra stress.

Her mum believed Adam was her adoring, loving husband, and Bianca was going to make sure she continued to think that till she was well out of the woods.

'Where's Adam?' May asked straight away. 'Parking the car?'

Bianca swallowed, smiled, then started on her newest invention. 'Actually, no, he couldn't be here with me, Mum. Your surprise visit has unfortunately coincided with a series of conferences in America Adam simply *had* to attend. He was wretchedly disappointed, but this trip was very important to his career at the university.'

'Oh, what a shame,' her Mum sighed. 'And I was so looking forward to seeing him again. I do so love that boy. I always knew he was the right one for you, Bianca. I'm just so glad that you finally realised it too. Still, maybe you and he can come over to Scotland some time in the near future. I'd love the rest of the family to meet him.'

'Er...yes, of course, Mum.' Bianca could not trust herself to say any more. Resentment that Adam had put her in this awkward position had begun to sizzle inside her again. She also bitterly resented the thought that she would have to lie like this for a whole fortnight while he was off having fun with his new lady love and not giving *her* a second thought!

'Let's get out of here,' she said, rather abruptly, and her mother gave her a sharp and far too intuitive look.

'There isn't anything wrong, is there, darling?'

Bianca found a dazzling smile from somewhere. 'Wrong? What could possibly be wrong?'

'I don't know...'

Bianca linked arms with her mother and dazzled some more. 'You silly billy! I haven't been this happy in years. We're going to have such fun this next fortnight, you and I. I've taken two weeks' holiday off work and we're going to paint Sydney red!'

Bianca started telling her mother all she had planned, and by the time they were on their way— the car had still coughed and spluttered before starting—that slight worry in her mother's eyes had totally disappeared. Thank God.

'What a lovely flat you live in,' her mother said as she walked out onto the balcony of Adam's unit an hour later.

'Yes, I suppose it is,' Bianca agreed with a degree of surprise. Really, she didn't care much about her surroundings, provided there was a shower and a toilet, a comfortable bed to sleep in and some kind of kitchen to cook in.

But, with her mother's comment, she took a fresh glance around at the spacious and modern unit, with its crisp white walls, brown leather furniture, plush sable-coloured carpet and marvellous aspect. They were only a couple of streets away from Collaroy Beach, and high enough to have an un-impeded view of the beach and the Pacific beyond.

Though not in the luxurious category, the two-bedroomed unit was very comfortable by anyone's standards.

'Do you own it or rent it?' Mrs Peterson called back over her shoulder.

Bianca bit her bottom lip at this question. Did Adam own it or rent it? She didn't know. She'd never asked and he'd never volunteered the information. She rather suspected he owned it, which was why he let her live here free. But she wasn't sure.

'It's...er...still being paid off,' she said carefully.

'It's lovely. But not really suitable for children.' Her mother walked back inside and into the kitchen, where Bianca was making them both a cup of tea. 'Are you planning on having a family soon?' she asked hopefully.

Bianca's heart squeezed tight. She knew what her mother was getting at. She wanted to be a grandmother before she died.

'Not just yet, Mum,' she returned, a little tautly.

'You do realise it might take you some time to get pregnant, with your periods the way they are?'

'Yes, I know.' Bianca was one of those girls who only had a few periods a year. When she'd been playing heavy sport she'd hardly had any. She'd always joked with her mother that if she ever fell pregnant she'd have to have the baby—no matter what the circumstances—because it might be the only baby she'd ever be blessed with!

Earlier this year she'd gone on the pill, in an effort to regulate things and boost her oestrogen level, but it had made her feel so yukky she'd stopped taking it three weeks back. She had no doubt that the artificial period which had naturally followed the next week would be the last period she would see for months.

She sighed her exasperation at her body, which had always been a source of frustration to her. She would have given anything to be an Amazon with big boobs, legs ten feet long and a period every month that you could set your clock by.

'You might have to take one of those fertility pills,' her mother said. 'Though that usually produces multiple births. You wouldn't want that.'

'God, no.' Bianca had trouble picturing herself coping with one baby at a time, let alone several.

'Does Adam want a big family?'

'Let's not talk about babies, Mum. Adam and I have only been married a few months after all. Do you want a biscuit with your tea? Dinner won't be for a couple of hours yet.'

Her mum took the hint and dropped the subject of babies, though not without first giving her a long, thoughtful look. Bianca suspected her silence on the subject was only temporary. She began to dread the coming fortnight.

The evening finally drew to a close. Her meal of Thai curried chicken and rice had been a surprising success, given her mother's tendency to cook plain food herself.

Bianca had also expected her mother to crash out early with jet lag, but she'd said she wanted to get her body onto Sydney time, so they'd watched the Friday night Ruth Rendell movie, which went on quite late, after which her mother had finally got ready for bed and taken her sleeping tablet.

Bianca made them both a cup of cocoa as a nightcap, and they were sitting on the sofa in front of the television, idly watching the late news and sipping their hot drinks, when an item came on covering the première earlier that evening of a new Australian movie.

Bianca started watching the segment rather cynically, thinking how like Hollywood the Australian movie industry was becoming. A whole lot of hype and not always that much quality!

There was the obligatory red carpet, the white stretch limousines, the screaming fans and, of course, the stars...glamorous women dressed in glitzy gowns and handsome men looking impossibly suave and sophisticated in superbly cut tuxedos. Such a false world, Bianca was thinking, when suddenly a very familiar face filled the screen.

A familiar face, yet *not* a familiar one. Bianca could hardly believe that was *her* Adam, in one of those superbly cut tuxedos, with one of those glamorous women on his arm dressed in a gold lamé gown cut right down to her navel.

'Isn't that Adam?' her mother said in a puzzled voice.

'Shh!' Bianca hissed, desperate to hear what the commentator was saying. She didn't stop to realise how damning his words might be to her story of her supposed husband being over in the US of A at a harmless conference.

'And here's Sophie La Salle arriving. Sophie has only a small part in this new and daring film, but one hopes that some smart producer will realise the public will want to see more of the glorious Sophie in future. Not that we aren't seeing quite a bit of her already here tonight. That's some dress, Sophie!

'It certainly seems to be appreciated by her very handsome escort. Can't say I recognise him. Perhaps he's one of the show's producers. Maybe we'll get a hint as to his identity later this evening at the post-première party. We'll keep you posted, folks.'

Furious disbelief exploded in Bianca's brain as she watched Adam slide an intimate arm around that disgustingly gorgeous creature's incredibly small waist. Or maybe it just looked small, she thought viciously, because of the size of the breasts above it, which not even the thick golden tresses spilling over them could begin to hide!

'Bianca, that *is* Adam, isn't it?' her mother was saying somewhere in Bianca's hazy background. Her whole focus was still fixed on the television screen and the way Adam was smiling into that woman's smugly beautiful face as he shepherded her into the theatre. She'd never realised before what a sexy smile he had. Or how handsome he was.

When had he grown that handsome, dammit?

'Bianca?' her mother prodded impatiently.

'Yes, it's Adam,' she bit out.

'But... But...'

'The bastard!' Bianca added savagely, no longer caring about anything but the rage flooding through her. And the jealousy. A black, black jealousy.

This last realisation had her jumping to her feet and pacing agitatedly around the room. She couldn't possibly be jealous. Being jealous was a symptom of loving someone. And she didn't love Adam. Not like that. It had to be a case of that selfish possessiveness Adam had accused her of, whereby she didn't want him herself but she didn't want anyone else to have him.

'Bianca,' her mother said firmly as she stood up and switched off the television set. 'Will you please stand still and tell me what's going on here?'

Bianca struggled to gather herself. And once she did she accepted that she would have to tell her mother the truth. She wasn't going to pretend that Adam had thrown her over for that blonde bombshell, though it felt as if he had. And she didn't like the feeling one bit!

'I'm sorry, Mum,' she said brusquely, 'but I haven't been strictly honest with you.'

'Well, that's pretty obvious! Adam is clearly not over in America at any conference, since he was

here in Sydney tonight, accompanying that...
that... actress... to the movies!'

'So it seems,' Bianca agreed through gritted teeth.

'My God, he's left you, hasn't he?' came her
mother's shocked conclusion. 'He's having an affair
with that... that... trollop!'

'That's the way it looks, I guess.'

'I can't believe it! I thought Adam was different.
It just shows that most men can't be trusted—especially where a beautiful woman is concerned. A
pretty girl only had to bat her eyes at your father
and he was a goner.'

Bianca's sigh was deep and weary. She'd heard
about her father's unfaithfulness at some length all
her life and didn't want another lecture on the male
sex's lack of moral fibre. She also wished to heaven
she'd never started this.

Time, she decided resignedly, for the truth.

Bianca was about to launch into a full confession
when the sound of a key rattling in the front door
lock distracted her.

Both women's eyes turned in time to see Adam
walk in, still in his tuxedo—although the bow tie
was now undone, suggesting it might have been removed at some stage during the evening. He looked
startled to see Bianca's mother standing in the
room.

He also still looked disturbingly handsome,
Bianca conceded, confusion in her heart. She
couldn't stop staring at him and wondering if she'd
really looked at him lately.

Her eyes swept over him now, taking in the adult Adam for perhaps the first time in years.

His face, though not classically formed, was undeniably *very* handsome: strong male features combined with intelligent grey eyes to project an impressive look of maturity and confidence. His dark brown hair, which he'd once worn far too long and wayward, was now superbly cut to fit his nicely shaped head. His mouth, she noticed, was just as nicely shaped, the bottom lip sensuously full.

Bianca liked nice mouths on men.

She frowned as she started having decidedly erotic thoughts, not so much about men's mouths in general, but Adam's in particular. Annoyed with herself, she dropped her eyes to follow the full length of Adam's frame, trying to find something she could happily criticise.

She found the dinner suit he was wearing—that very expensive-looking, silk blend, satanic black and devilishly attractive dinner suit.

Most men would look good in that outfit, she decided waspishly. It was like a magic wand. Pop it on any male and *poof*, its inhabitant would become instantly glamorous and gorgeous—a bit like Cinderella did once her fairy godmother had garbed her in that beautiful ball dress and glass slippers.

That suit was better than any fairy godmother's wand!

Bianca's now scornful gaze rested on the undoubtedly padded shoulders, which would account for Adam's suddenly superb shape. Not a wrinkle creased either sleeve, nor the long, elegant trousers, seemingly housing equally long, elegant legs.

Bianca scowled as she tried to recall the last time she'd seen Adam's legs in the buff. No image came to mind. Yet she must have, she supposed, either in shorts, or some time around the unit—though he wasn't into shorts, and that red dressing gown he always wore covered a hell of a lot of him.

Her irritation grew as she realised that, although they lived near a beach, she'd never gone swimming with him, so she didn't know what he looked like in a cossie. How *was* it, she puzzled furiously, that they'd never gone swimming together?

His startled grey eyes met her glaring ones, and he gave the wall clock a darting glance. It was just on midnight.

Cinderella, it seemed, Bianca decided with savage sarcasm, had left the ball and finally come home.

CHAPTER FIVE

It only took Adam a few seconds to get the picture. Bianca's mother must have flown in earlier than intended, and his coming home had completely obliterated whatever outrageous story Bianca had told her to explain his absence from the marital home.

He almost laughed. It was a fitting end to a bloody awful night and a bloody awful week. The only good thing to come out of it was that he'd spent each night at the casino, winning incredible sums of money. Incredible because he'd bet recklessly, with no real system. His mind had been too full of Bianca to concentrate on a system, or even a proper staking plan.

Ironic that he'd come back, trying to do the right thing by her, his conscience having finally got the better of him, only to drop her right in it, obviously. He gave her an apologetic shrug which was met with a glare so fierce he was taken aback.

Good God, what *had* she told her mother about their marriage? He shuddered to think.

'Hello, Mrs Peterson,' he said with a sheepish smile. 'You're looking well.' Which she did.

She'd also always looked upon him with favour.

Till this moment . . .

'Hello, indeed,' she returned stiffly. 'And you're looking guilty. I hope you've finally seen the error of your ways and come to beg Bianca's forgiveness.'

'Pardon?' He shot Bianca a please-help-me glance, only to have those dagger eyes of hers cutting him to shreds again.

'There's no use playing Mr Innocent, Adam,' Bianca snapped. 'We saw you on the late-night news, escorting darling Sophie to the première of that movie tonight.'

Oh, he thought, and had to smother a laugh again. That would certainly have blotted his copy-book, if he was supposed to be Bianca's loving husband. Which, no doubt, he still was. Bianca would not have backed down and told her mother she'd lied. That was not her usual *modus operandi* at all. She would have plunged further into the mire of more deceit and deception rather than confess all.

Admittedly, one look at her mother's stern and disapproving face was even making *him* feel guilty and uncomfortable. And he hadn't done *anything*!

'I tried to cover for your absence by telling Mum you were at an overseas conference,' Bianca raged on, blue eyes flashing and cheeks flushed a bright red. 'But you rather blew my excuse out of the water with your very public behaviour with that disgusting woman tonight. The least you could have done was conduct your affair behind closed doors, not flaunt it for all the world to see. You've made me look a fool, Adam, and I will not have it!'

Adam could hardly believe what he was hearing, and astonishment over Bianca's attack mixed with astonishment over her demeanour.

He'd never seen her so angry. Or so damned beautiful! This level of temper tantrum did become her. And he didn't think he'd ever seen her wearing such a feminine skirt before—certainly not one which rustled around her legs with each movement she made. He was momentarily distracted by the thought of how easily he could slide his hands up her legs with a skirt like that.

'I want you to leave!' she stormed on. 'Get your clothes or whatever you've come for and just go!'

Adam dragged his attention back up to Bianca's scorn-filled eyes, his fantasy fleeing in the face of reality. Any amusement vanished, his heart hardening against her. Who in hell did she think she was, making him look this bad in her mother's eyes?

He decided two could play at this game. After all, he'd vowed never to let her use him ever again. He'd warned her too. She should have listened to him.

'I have no intention of going anywhere, Bianca. This is my home, and you're my wife. I'm back and I won't be leaving again.'

To give her credit, she didn't turn a hair at his counter-attack. He had to admire her spirit. Bianca never knew when she was beaten.

'Really?' she snorted. 'Might I ask what happened to cause this change of heart? Last weekend you told me you were leaving me for good. You even said you were going to marry that Sophie person. Though God knows why. Men don't marry women like Sophie, you know. They just screw them.'

Adam heard Bianca's mother gasp of shock but he didn't think Bianca had. Her blood was too far up. He couldn't make up his mind whether she was mad at being found out in more lies, or just mad at being thwarted. He decided to thwart her some more. He liked seeing her like this. It was almost as if she cared about him.

'Why should you care what I do, Bianca? You never loved me. You only married me to make your mother happy. Why don't you admit it?'

'Is that true, Bianca?' her mother intervened, her expression and her voice holding intense shock and disapproval.

'No!' Bianca denied hotly.

Adam wasn't going to let her get away with that. 'Then you're telling me you *do* love me?'

'I've always loved you, Adam,' she insisted, a guilty red heightening the colour in her cheeks.

He knew she was playing with words, using the love she felt for him as a friend to mean another kind of love—the *only* kind he wanted from her. Her lie infuriated him. 'No kidding?' he said coldly. 'Did you love me when you went away to a motel last weekend with another man?'

'Bianca!' her mother gasped, looking totally appalled now. 'You didn't!'

'Oh, yes, she did,' Adam swept on while Bianca's mouth flapped open. 'His name is Derek. He's a professional weight-lifter. Wall-to-wall muscles. You must know your daughter's predilection for beefy men, May. She's never hidden it.'

'I . . . I thought she was over that. I thought she'd finally seen some sense.'

'Who are you to talk?' Bianca burst in. 'You with your busty blondes. Sophie wasn't the only one, Mum. There's been a whole line of overblown blonde bimbos before her!'

'You mean you noticed?' Adam tossed back with blithe indifference.

'Hard not to when you paraded them through here for me to see.'

His laugh was harshly dry. 'Careful, Bianca, or I'll begin to think you're jealous.'

'Over *you*?' she sneered.

Adam hadn't thought she could hurt him any more than she already had. But he'd been wrong. He looked at her now and hated her—hated her with a passion which was as annoyingly sexual as his love had been.

'She's exaggerating, May. They were just students I was giving some extra tutoring to.'

'What in?' Bianca scoffed. 'The *Kama Sutra*?'

'No. I leave those particular lessons up to you,' he countered icily, glad to see shamed colour sweep up her neck. 'I swear to you, May, that I haven't been unfaithful since my marriage to your daughter.'

Which was technically true, since Bianca had only announced their married state last weekend. He hadn't taken Sophie out all week. She'd wanted to get her beauty sleep for tonight's première. Neither had they made love tonight. He'd left her at the post-première party, making eyes at an American director.

'Not that I haven't been tempted,' he added snakily. 'My loving wife hasn't been giving me any attention lately. It's been so long since she slept with me, I can't remember what it was like.'

Bianca's eyes narrowed to savage slits. 'Hard to sleep with you when you're hardly ever home!'

'I'm home now,' he said coolly, and watched with bitter amusement as Bianca struggled to control her temper.

'Are you saying that you still love me?' she asked archly. 'That all those other women meant nothing to you? Sophie included?'

'Absolutely nothing. It's always been you, Bianca,' he said, hating himself as his voice shook slightly. 'You're the only woman I've ever loved, or ever will love.'

He cursed himself when her eyes widened, as did her mouth. Slowly. Smilingly. Damn, but she was actually looking smug now. Adam's teeth clenched down hard in his jaw. He was going to wipe that triumphant smirk off her face if it was the last thing he did.

'Darling,' she said with simpering sweetness, and came forward to give him a mock hug and a mock kiss on the cheek.

'Darling,' he returned grittily, and, taking her chin in a forceful grip, turned her face so that he could kiss her full on the mouth.

He wasn't a fool, however. He kept his tongue to himself, so that she couldn't bite it, revelling instead in the feel of her shocked lips and flinching body. God, but it felt good to be able to kiss her like this, knowing she was hating it yet unable to do a damned thing about it. Her lies held her captive beneath his lips.

His satisfaction was savage, and he began to understand the attraction of putting a woman over one's knee and paddling her backside. It would certainly satisfy that deeply primitive need a man had to dominate and control his woman by physical force—especially when that woman was as spirited and defiant as Bianca.

When he lifted his mouth he was surprised to find she was looking up at him with a type of bewildered respect in her eyes. It was a look he could easily get used to, he decided, so he took her firmly by the shoulders and kissed her again. This time he even had the temerity to slide his tongue between her startled lips, hoping like hell that this uncharacteristic respect would last a few more seconds.

Nevertheless, he kept this second kiss brief, for the feel of his own tongue in her mouth pushed him quickly to an edge of desire that was as terrifying as it was intoxicating.

He knew then that it would not be the last time he kissed her this night. Not by a long shot.

'Oh, how romantic,' Bianca's mother was sniffling from the sidelines as he surfaced.

'Say a single word,' he rasped, when Bianca sucked in a sharp breath, 'and I'll tell her the real truth. I swear it!'

Her mouth snapped shut, but her eyes spoke volumes.

'Why don't you go to bed, May?' he suggested, with far more calm than he was feeling. 'You must be very tired. Bianca and I will be just fine now. I think I have your visit to thank for her finally seeing some sense where our marriage is concerned. We were heading for disaster before you arrived.'

'So I can see!'

'I didn't do a thing with Derek last weekend, Mum,' Bianca insisted, sounding like a naughty little girl trying to defend herself, despite her hand being caught in the cookie jar. Adam just stopped himself from shaking his head. Would her lies never stop?

'I...I was just trying to make Adam jealous, to make him see how it felt to have someone you loved looking at someone else.'

As if she knew what that was like, Adam thought viciously. She'd never really loved anyone in her life!

'It seems you've been two very silly people,' May said. 'You're far too old to play silly games like that.'

'I couldn't agree more, May,' Adam said. 'And there'll be no more games. I promise.'

'I'm glad to hear that.' A yawn took her by surprise and she apologised.

'Go to bed, May.'

'Yes, I *am* very tired. And I took a sleeping tablet just before you came in. But no more arguing, mind. I couldn't bear it.'

He wrapped an arm tightly around Bianca's shoulders, pulling her close and throwing her a sickeningly adoring look. 'I'll be too busy kissing her for that.'

May smiled her approval. 'You do that, Adam. It certainly seems to work. I don't recall ever seeing Bianca this subdued. 'Night, darling,' she directed at the stiffly held and no doubt smouldering female by Adam's side. 'I'm so happy you two have made up.'

'Smile,' he hissed under his breath as he kept up his own mock adoration.

Bianca smiled and said goodnight to her mother.

The guest bedroom door was hardly closed when she rounded on him, wrenching out of his arms and spitting fury. 'How *dare* you?'

'Keep it down, Bianca,' he drawled softly. 'You don't want your mother to hear, do you?'

She took two handfuls of his lapels and dragged him into the kitchen. 'You had no right to tell her about Derek and make it sound like I was an adulteress! I know you don't think much of my morals but I do have some. And I would never, ever commit adultery!'

'Gee whiz, I'm glad to hear that, Bianca, especially now that we're married.'

'Don't be ridiculous. You know we're not really married.'

'We are for the next fortnight. And I aim to enjoy the plusses as well as suffer the negatives.'

'En—enjoy the plusses?' she echoed, all the colour in her face fading. 'What do you mean by that?'

Adam wasn't sure himself, but he was getting some pretty exciting ideas. 'What do you think I mean? I might not still be in love with you, Bianca, but I still fancy you. Since I can't have Sophie or any of my other ''blonde bimbos'' while your mother's here, I'll make do with you.'

He rather enjoyed her look of stunned amazement. At least it wasn't revulsion. 'You wouldn't dare,' she croaked.

Wouldn't he?

Too damn right he would.

His laugh was low and dark. 'Try me.'

'I won't let you.'

'Won't you?' He arched an eyebrow and boldly stroked a slow hand down over her left breast.

She jumped back, but not before he felt her bare nipple peak hard against her blouse. Bianca rarely wore a bra. Her involuntary response sent an electric charge all through him, despite the fact that he knew it wasn't for him especially. He'd always known she was a highly sexed creature.

She was staring at him again as though she didn't recognise him. 'I . . . I don't want you like that,' she said, as though trying to convince herself.

Adam merely smiled. She no longer had the power to hurt him with that silly statement. He'd crossed back over the line from love to hate once more, and he was finding that a much more daring and quite ruthless emotion. He could make her want him. He felt sure of it.

But he knew if he said as much to her she would fight her feelings. And him. Bianca was as stubborn as she was proud.

His shrug was nonchalant. 'No matter. Just lie back and think of your mother's health and happiness. Or think of *mine*. After all, I'm your best friend, aren't I? And you love me to death. Or so you've told me often enough. You wouldn't want me to suffer because of your lies, would you?'

'Suffer?' she echoed blankly.

'Contrary to your popular opinion of me, I am a highly sexed man who views a whole fortnight's celibacy with something akin to horror. If you wish to stop me straying, you'll have to keep me happy in bed.'

'I should have told Mum the truth,' she wailed.

'Perhaps,' he agreed. 'But it's too late now.'

'It's never too late,' she pouted.

His eyes dropped to her lips and he began thinking of all the ways he wanted them.

'Oh, I think it is, Bianca,' he said. And, drawing her forcefully into his arms, he started on the first one.

CHAPTER SIX

BIANCA could not believe what was happening. Adam was kissing her and she was enjoying it. No, not enjoying. That was the wrong word. She felt too confused for real enjoyment.

But there was no denying that her body was responding to the hungry passion of Adam's lips and the steely embrace she was wrapped in. It was automatically melting into him, avidly welcoming the invasion of that demanding tongue and even wanting more.

He whirled her in his arms, lifting her feet slightly off the floor as he strode back into the lounge room and pulled her down with him onto the large sofa, kissing her all the while.

Bianca felt dazed and dazzled by this new and very exciting Adam. She had never dreamt he could be like this. And, while her mind was still struggling to come to terms with this unexpected side to his character, her body kept responding with instinctive delight. She'd always loved forceful men, loved it when they took charge of lovemaking, sweeping her along with the strength and power of their male passions.

He angled her body beside him, her back pressed into the squashy leather of the sofa. His mouth on hers continued its hungry demands, making her blood sing and her head whirl. Desire for more contact had her lifting her right leg up to lie along his. When one of his hands started sliding up that leg all she could think about was how far it was before he reached its zenith.

Every ounce of her concentration was soon focused on that travelling hand as it moved slowly up her thigh. She moaned softly when his fingers finally fluttered against the lace edge of her panties. His mouth burst from hers and they both drew in deep, ragged breaths. Breathing heavily, he buried his face in her neck and his hand moved on.

It was under the elastic now, finding moist folds and electric places. Bianca began quivering with pleasure and expectation. Yes, touch me there, she willed him. And there. Oh, yes, that's it. Keep doing that. She moaned her excitement, plus her frustration.

Please don't let him stop, she prayed wildly. Please . . .

He stopped, his hand withdrawing as he rolled from her and stood up, coolly arranging her clothes before raking his own ruffled hair from his face. 'Not here,' he said, his eyes oddly cold as they moved over her flushed and flustered face. 'And not like this.'

He was gone before she could assemble her thoughts into words, stalking off down to the master bedroom. Bianca scrambled off the sofa, her heart still thudding heavily, her body screaming with thwarted desire.

She chased after him, only to find him taking off his expensive jacket and hanging it carefully in the wardrobe. He looked totally unconcerned about what had just transpired between them, as though it were nothing out of the ordinary.

Yet it was. It was very much out of the ordinary—both *his* actions and her *re*actions.

'Adam, I...' She hesitated, distracted by the sight of him flicking open the buttons of his white dress shirt then stripping it back off his shoulders. Nicely tanned and very broad shoulders, she noted, attached to an equally broad chest which looked toned beneath the smattering of dark curls.

He walked over and threw the shirt in the cane clothes basket in the corner, the movement highlighting the rippling muscles in his back and arms.

'Have you been doing weights?' she asked abruptly, her voice sounding almost resentful, as though he had no right to be doing things like that behind her back.

A wry smile hovered around his nicely shaped mouth as he turned to look at her. 'Glad to see you still have your priorities right, Bianca. But, yes, I've been doing weights. *And* working out. I have been on a regular basis for over ten years now.'

'Oh,' was all she could say, her gaze genuinely admiring as he walked towards the *en suite* bathroom.

'Care to join me?' he drawled, sending a cool glance over his shoulder at her.

Bianca blinked. *Did* she? Her head was pounding, as was her heart. Suddenly she didn't know where she stood with Adam any more, either with her own feelings or his. He was like a stranger to her...a very sexy stranger who was throwing her for a loop.

She wanted him. Oh, yes, she wanted him like mad.

But where would it all end? An affair with the Adam she'd used to know—or thought she had—would probably have headed towards marriage and babies, to a secure relationship with love and commitment. Because that old Adam had really, truly loved her.

But this new, totally alien Adam was a different prospect indeed. There was a coldness about him, a hardness which she couldn't explain or understand. Had Sophie thrown him over for someone else tonight? Turned him into an instant woman-hater? Bianca could hardly believe how ruthlessly he'd turned this sham of a marriage against her, using it to force kisses on her and then force himself on her.

Oh, come now, Bianca. The voice of brutal honesty intruded. Force? He wasn't forcing you out there on that sofa. You'd have let him do damned well anything and begged him for more.

What a mind-blowing realisation! How had Adam suddenly captured her sexual interest? Where had the spark come from? The chemistry?

It was this new and insidiously compelling chemistry which drew her into the bathroom. She stood there, watching him strip off to total nudity, a lump forming in her throat as she saw why perhaps he'd hurt her so much all those years ago. Yet he wasn't even aroused!

That stunned her. How could he not be aroused after what he'd done to her out there?

'Like what you see, Bianca?' he drawled from across the room.

'Yes...' It wasn't in Bianca's nature to be sexually coy, but the admission was made on a husky note, forced out of dry lips from a very dry throat.

A coldly rueful smile gave his mouth a strange look as he slowly crossed the distance between them. 'Then what are you waiting for, darling?' he asked, in a mockingly sardonic voice which scraped across every nerve-ending she owned. 'I'll bet you weren't this slow to get out of your clothes your first time with dear old Derek. Or is it that you want me to undress you? Do you have a fetish for your lovers stripping you? Is that it?'

Bianca had never felt more torn. She wanted to tell him to go to hell, show him she wasn't going to let him get away with treating her like this. Instead, she slid her arms up around his neck, reached up on tiptoe and kissed him, pressing herself against his splendid nakedness.

'Yes,' she breathed against his suddenly frozen lips. 'Yes, I have a fetish for my lovers stripping me.'

Adam swore under his breath as his flesh leapt. Damn, but she was trying to turn the tables on him, trying to take control. He wasn't having any of that.

Dampening down his desire with another supreme effort of will, he extricated her arms from around his neck and stepped back slightly so that he could begin on the buttons of her blouse.

She was taken aback by his seeming control, he could see, her eyes wide on him as he undressed her with casual aplomb. The sight of her perfect little breasts with their large, hard nipples endangered more than his physical control, but he kept going, sliding the zip of her skirt down and easing the garment over her slender hips to pool on the white-tiled floor.

Now all that separated her from total nudity before him was a scrap of pink satin and lace. He thought of where his fingers had already been as he peeled the panties down her athletic legs, of her hot, wet, pulsing core. It was almost too much for him. It was certainly too much for his repressed but aching flesh, which sprang to life, rearing up with primal urgency.

Whirling abruptly from her, he strode over to turn on the shower taps, standing with his back to her while he adjusted the temperature and battled to get himself at least marginally under control.

At last he felt sufficiently in charge of his
emotions—and his body—to face her once more.

Bianca was shivering by the time he returned to
draw her with him under the hot spray. Not from
cold. From a dizzying excitement. And an exquisite
expectation.

Yet beside her almost blind arousal lay a bitter
resentment that Adam was not similarly turned on.
She wanted to see him as mindlessly impassioned
as she was. His cool composure seemed to be em-
phasising her own lack of control, her own wanton
willingness to surrender herself totally to his casual
and rather cold sexual demands.

Where was the Adam who'd once followed her
around like an adoring puppy? Who'd have lain his
life at her feet if she'd wanted him to?

Gone. She had to accept it. Replaced by this cool,
enigmatic stranger who was at this moment doing
the most wicked things to her body with a bar of
soap, turning her this way and that beneath the
heated spray of water, sending her mad with desire
as he teased aching nipples, massaged trembling
buttocks and throbbing thighs.

She was shaking by the time he snapped the water
off and began towelling her dry. He carried her back
into the bedroom, for which she was grateful—she
knew she wouldn't have been able to walk. Her eyes
clung to him as he laid her down on the bed, and
for the first time she saw a spark of conscience, a
moment of doubt over what he was doing.

For Bianca, it was too late for that. She no longer wanted his conscience, or his doubts. She only wanted him, inside her, expelling this almost hateful need from her body. She'd never felt this strung up, or this desperate. Her hands snaked round his neck, her fingers interlinking as she drew his mouth and body down on top of hers.

Her legs opened to wrap tightly around him, her buttocks lifting from the mattress till his flesh fell with driving hardness into the softness of her woman's body. With a powerful thrust which took her breath away he was suddenly there, filling her completely. He cupped her face with his hands and stared down into her wild, wide eyes, watching her while he began moving with a voluptuous and powerful rhythm.

Bianca squeezed her eyes shut against the shame of Adam seeing her so lost to everything but her body's demands. Her mouth fell open as she felt her climax begin to build. She gasped her pleasure, then groaned her torment, grimacing when the knife-edge of tension tightened its grip on her nerve-endings.

The knowledge that he wanted to coldly watch her come brought one last burst of defiance, and her eyes flew open. But she was too late, those tortured nerve-endings giving up the ghost, bringing a twisted cry to her lips as her flesh shattered into a thousand electric spasms. Her contractions were fierce and strong around his flesh, the pleasure unbelievable.

The look of dark triumph on his face frightened Bianca at first, but then his mouth gasped wide with agonised ecstasy, his release as cataclysmic as her own.

'Oh, God, Bianca!' he cried out, collapsing on top of her, burying his face in her hair. 'Bianca...'

She had never heard her name called out with such emotion, or such despair. It moved her unbearably and she gathered him close, instinctively trying to soothe him. The certainty that he still loved her, despite his earlier denial, evoked the most incredibly warm feelings inside her. It made what they had just shared something much more wonderful than anything she'd ever experienced before.

But no sooner had she hugged him tight than he was wrenching himself out of her arms and abruptly withdrawing from her body. The obscenity he used as he rolled over onto his back made her flinch.

'What is it?' she asked, levering herself up on one elbow to look down at him. 'What's wrong?'

'Nothing,' he bit out, slanting her an angry glance. 'I hope,' he added viciously.

'What are you saying?'

'I'm saying I didn't use anything just then, dammit. And you made no move to stop me. Not once!'

'Oh,' she said softly, her stomach flipping over as she lay back down again. There was no use making excuses. She simply hadn't thought of it.

'Yes, *oh*!' he growled, rolling over onto his side to glare down at her. 'Hell, Bianca, I hope you're not in the habit of getting carried away like that. I know you're on the pill, but that's not the point these days, is it?'

Bianca opened her mouth to tell him that actually she *wasn't* on the pill. But she quickly closed it again, sensing that there was nothing to be gained by the admission. The odds of her falling pregnant on this one-off occasion were so remote as to be almost negligible.

But she had a feeling Adam wouldn't be too pleased with the news of even the slightest possibility. He didn't look too pleased all round.

'You always said the reason you never told your boyfriends you were on the pill was because you wanted them to always use a condom,' he ranted. 'You've always claimed to be fanatical about safe sex. What just happened rather proves you're not infallible when it comes to being Miss Protection Perfect, wouldn't you say?'

Bianca could feel her own blood pressure rising, but she battled to remain calm. 'I have never, ever *not* practised safe sex before tonight, Adam,' she stated firmly. 'And, contrary to your opinion of me, I have not had that many lovers over the years. Barely a handful. Can you say the same?'

'Maybe not, but I can assure you practising safe sex is an automatic way of life with me.'

'You've always used a condom?'

'Too darned right I have.'

'Then why didn't you tonight?' she counter-challenged.

He pressed his lips tightly together, his eyes seething with resentment at her attempt to make him admit he'd got as carried away as she had. 'I guess at the back of my mind I knew you were on the pill,' he muttered at last. 'And maybe, at the back of my mind, I just didn't damned well want to!'

'And maybe *I* had the same damned good reasons!' she threw back at him. 'But be assured I want you to use something in future, because I don't trust you any more than you trust me, Mr Protection *Im*perfect!'

Bianca was shocked when Adam started smiling down at her. It was a wickedly knowing smile, which sent a prickle of apprehension down her spine.

'What are you smiling at?' she snapped. And where had his anger gone to, dammit? She liked him angry. It made her feel safer than when he was... like this.

'At you, Bianca,' he drawled, and reached out to play idly with her nearest nipple.

Bianca was shocked when it sprang to attention with appalling swiftness. Stunned, she knocked his hand away and sat up. 'What do you think you're doing?' she asked shakily.

'What you just gave me permission to do,' he said, sitting up as well.

'I did no such thing.'

'Yes, you did. You asked me to use protection *in future*, which suggests you're expecting a repeat performance. I think the future, my darling wife of the next fortnight...' he murmured thickly as he reached out to play with both her breasts at the same time. 'The future...has already arrived.'

Bianca gasped when he took her shoulders and pushed her back against the pillows, straddling her and effectively pinning her to the mattress. Her cry of outrage was muffled by his kiss, her eyes rounding when Adam used his hands to find her body's most electric and seductive places.

'Hush,' he said when she moaned a pained protest. 'You don't want to wake your mother, do you?'

He kissed her again for an interminable time, only removing his mouth when she no longer had the will to scream—and when he had other uses for her lips.

CHAPTER SEVEN

ADAM carried the breakfast tray into the bedroom, his mouth tightening as his eyes lit upon Bianca's still naked form sprawled face-down across the bed. Her lovely long black hair, no longer confined in that purple thing, was spread out in tangled abandon against the cool, creamy sheets. She looked the picture of erotic decadence—utterly spent from an orgy of sensual delights.

If only her mother could see her now...

But Mrs Peterson was still safely asleep, that sleeping tablet doing a good job. Not that it was all that late. Only eight.

Adam placed the tray carefully on top of the bedside table, sat down on the side of the bed and stared down at the delicious curve of Bianca's spine. He could not resist the temptation, and bent to kiss the small of her back before running his tongue-tip slowly upwards.

'Don't,' she groaned, arching away from him and then rolling over, her arms flopping wide, her eyes still shut.

His gut contracted as his gaze raked over her beautifully formed, perfectly toned little body.

Bianca had always bemoaned her small breasts and her lack of height, but to him she was just right.

He adored the shape of her slender curves, loved the way each breast fitted neatly into the palm of his hand, revelled in the fact that she was so much smaller than he was. And correspondingly less strong.

His heart lurched as he thought of how he'd forced the issue with her last night, through his superior strength alone. He wasn't proud of that fact, but, damn it all, she hadn't objected for long. She'd been more than willing to give him what he wanted in the end.

And he'd wanted so much—all those things he'd thought of doing with her over the years and never been able to. Well, he'd done most of them now, and it hadn't dampened his passion for her one bit. Or his love, for that matter. He loved her more than ever. Wanted her more than ever. Hell, he wanted her to be his for forever. Wanted her to be his *real* wife.

But he knew Bianca would never be his, or any other man's, for forever. He was damned lucky to have got this far with her. Her abandoned behaviour with him last night was nothing out of the ordinary, not even those bittersweet moments of total surrender, when any man who didn't know her might have thought she must love him to allow such torrid intimacies.

But Adam knew the truth. A set of unusual circumstances had allowed him to tap into Bianca's Achilles' heel—sex—and she was simply running true to form.

Once sexually attracted to a man, she always quickly became infatuated, even obsessed. She lived and breathed that man. Nothing was too good for him, in bed and out.

But only for a time. Eventually she would begin to find flaws in what she'd once thought was a perfect male specimen. Sometimes it was the man who opted out first, probably because she'd begun to pick him to pieces. At other times she did the breaking up herself.

Oddly enough, the longest lasting of her lovers had been one who hadn't treated her very well at all. The bastard had actually boasted to Adam one day that his success with women was because he lived by the adage 'Treat 'em mean, keep 'em keen'.

Adam personally found that theory distasteful. But, damn it all, it seemed to work. Where had being the good guy ever got him with Bianca? Bloody nowhere. Yet as soon as he'd started standing up to her, and treating her as if he was a selfish, macho stud with nothing to lose, she'd fallen into his hands like a ripe peach. It was perverse in the extreme, but who was he to question the road to sexual success?

And he *was* being sexually successful with her. His loins leapt as he thought of the number of times he'd had her the previous night. Hell, he'd lost count.

Having her body might not be everything. He'd always wanted the complete woman—body and soul. But sex with Bianca went a long way to making him feel infinitely better about all the years he'd wasted futilely trying to win her heart.

He saw now that she was not capable of loving a man that way. *Any* man. Her relationships were based on lust. Once the intensity of her desire began to fade—which was inevitable—the relationship was dead in the water. Adam knew that this new desire of hers for him would not last. It never did.

But, meantime, he aimed to take full advantage of that desire.

He would have to be careful never to hope for more, however. Bianca had hurt him more than enough for one lifetime. To set himself up for added pain would be insane.

No, he wasn't going back to being stupid old Adam, boring best friend and doormat. He was going to stay being the man who'd shocked her into responding to him last night, the selfish stud who took without asking, who came and went without getting permission, who kept secrets from her and never, ever allowed himself to be taken for granted.

'Wake up, Bianca,' he said brusquely.

Her eyes fluttered but remained sleepily shut while she yawned, then stretched with voluptuous sensuality. Bianca's naked body had been bad enough. Her naked body moving like that was too much for Adam. He scooped her up and set her down on the carpet, smacking her hard on the bottom as he propelled her towards the bathroom.

'Hey, that hurt!' she protested, rubbing those
gloriously pouty buttocks of hers as she glared over
her shoulder at him.

'Good,' he pronounced. 'Now get that butt of
yours into the shower. It's after eight and I've
brought you some breakfast.'

She half turned, an incredulous smile on her face.
'You brought me breakfast?'

Adam made a mental note never to do such a
stupid thing again. 'If you can call muesli and
orange juice breakfast. But don't get used to it. I
thought you might need an energy boost after last
night,' he finished drily.

'Oh...'

The memory of the night flickered across her
face, bringing with it a faint trace of worry, he
thought. Or was it shame?

No, not shame, Adam conceded ruefully. Bianca
would never be ashamed of what she did in bed.
She thought of sex as a beautiful and natural expression of the attraction between a man and a
woman. There were no taboos in her mind. She was
always scathing of people who tried to make sex
into something wicked and dirty. Sick, she called
them.

That momentary cloud quickly cleared from her
wide blue eyes, replaced by a soft look which
twisted Adam's heart. Damn, but she was so good
at that, looking at him with the innocence of a
child. There again, she *was* a child in some ways,
always wanting fun and excitement, never wanting

the things a grown woman wanted—except in one department.

'Adam,' she said softly.

'What?'

'Thank you.'

'For what? Breakfast?'

'No. For coming back last night. You...you did it for me, didn't you? You wouldn't have had any idea Mum was already here. You left that Sophie female and came back to help me out.'

Well, of course he had! But he couldn't tell her that, could he? If he did, soon she'd start thinking of him again as good old Adam—loyal life-saver and breakfast-bringer.

He let his eyes drift over her with lazy amusement. 'Actually, Bianca, I hate to disillusion you, but I came back last night to pick up my books to take to the races today. I can't operate my system without them.'

She blinked her surprise before hurt darkened her eyes. 'Oh,' she said. 'Oh, I see.' She stiffened, and suddenly seemed to realise she was standing stark naked before him, her hands moving to cover herself. 'Sorry,' she muttered unhappily. 'My mistake.' And she hurried into the bathroom, shutting the door behind her.

Adam steeled himself against the automatic self-hate which flooded his heart. So he'd hurt her. Deliberately hurt her. So what? This was self-survival, here. He could not afford to wear his heart on his sleeve with her any more. He had to distance himself from this futile loving which had obsessed him most of his emotional life.

Lust was what he was going to concentrate on from now on, for in the long run that was all Bianca responded to. Real love she scorned as weakness. He could not afford to be weak with her if he wanted to keep her sexual interest. Which he did. Hell, a man would have to be mad not to want a repeat performance of last night. There were other Bianca fantasies he hadn't lived yet as well, and he aimed to live every one of them in the coming fortnight.

Oh, yes . . . his days of being a push-over were well and truly gone!

Bianca found herself crying under the shower. She had never felt this confused before. Or this vulnerable. Or this hurt.

The reason, of course, was Adam. Not the Adam she'd known and loved all her life, but the stranger sitting on that bed.

Last night, when he'd made love to her that first time and called out her name, she'd been so sure he still loved her. Even afterwards, when his lovemaking had become incredibly daring and increasingly demanding, she'd still felt confident that it *was* lovemaking and not just having sex. She could have sworn she'd felt a very special passion in every kiss, every caress.

Now she wasn't so sure. My God, the way he'd looked at her just then, the way he'd spoken to her.

He'd made her feel so...*unloved*.

More tears streamed down her face, which wasn't like her at all. The thought that she might have fallen in love with Adam at the same time he'd fallen *out* of love with *her* was distressing in the extreme.

And so frustrating.

It just wasn't fair!

But when had life—or love—been fair? she wondered with a degree of cynicism. Her own mother had married a man she'd loved to death, only to have him be chronically unfaithful to her. Bianca had always believed she was tarred with the same brush as her father, because she'd imagined herself deeply in love several times, only to fall out of love within a few months. She'd obviously always confused sexual attraction with love.

Bianca frowned. Since that had always been the case, then why should what she was feeling for Adam be any different? Maybe it, too, was just a sexual attraction and would wear off after a while?

She could not deny that seeing Adam on the television in that dashing tuxedo and on the arm of the stunning Sophie had lifted the wool from her eyes where his physical attractions were concerned. She'd begun looking at him with new eyes last night, and discovered an Adam she'd had no idea existed—an Adam who was more like the type of man she usually went for. Tall, well-built, strong and very macho.

Bianca sighed and switched off the shower. Even to her own ears that sounded awfully shallow. Yet hadn't she already decided this week that she *was* shallow? It was no wonder Adam no longer loved her. Living with her this past year had probably opened his eyes to the real Bianca, with all her shallowness and sexual superficiality.

Still, he didn't seem to mind *sampling* that sexual superficiality, did he? she thought savagely as she rubbed herself dry. He had taken outrageous advantage of her last night. He'd taken outrageous liberties as well! No doubt he expected more of the same tonight, and for the rest of her mother's stay.

Bianca's heart began to pound at the prospect. As much as she would have liked to feel outrage, all she felt was an excited anticipation. Tonight could not come quickly enough.

Bianca was not a girl to keep lashing herself over her own faults. Very well ... so she was sexually shallow—weak as water where the pleasures of the flesh were concerned. It wasn't entirely her fault this time. Who would have believed that the gawky boy who'd taken her virginity with such appalling ineptitude would develop into such a fantastic lover?

Jealousy re-erupted when she thought of him doing all those things he'd done to her with Sophie. She could just about tolerate his not loving her, but she was not going to tolerate another woman in his life. Not while *she* was in his bed. No way!

Bianca sashed a huge cream towel around her and stormed back out into the bedroom, her hands coming to rest on her hips as she ground to a halt.

'I want to know about Sophie!' she demanded hotly.

Adam glanced up from where he was still sitting on the edge of the bed, sipping *her* glass of orange juice. 'What about her?' His bland tone infuriated her.

'I hope you don't think you're going to be juggling the two of us. When I take a lover, I demand his exclusive attention.'

His eyebrows lifted, but his expression remained irritatingly casual. 'How nice for you. But I'm not your lover. I'm your pretend husband.'

'Same thing.'

'Oh, no, Bianca. Not at all. But, if it makes you feel better, be assured I won't be sleeping with Sophie during these two weeks. I don't think your mother would approve of my being absent from our marital bed at night, do you? And Sophie is not a day-time person. Besides, why would I want Sophie when you're being so accommodating?'

Bianca squirmed a little as she recalled just how accommodating she'd been. But any embarrassment was quickly replaced by a burst of defiance. Why should she feel ashamed of what they'd done together? Adam clearly didn't.

Bianca had never been one to abide by those double standards where sex was concerned, and she wasn't about to start now. Being a hypocrite was not her style.

She'd wanted Adam to make love to her last night and wasn't going to pretend differently this morning—even if he was turning out to be a very different Adam from the one she'd always thought she'd known so well. This new Adam was not at all sweet, or touchingly in love with her. She doubted he was in love with any woman, the selfish, sexy rat!

This realisation brought with it a sudden thought, and she eyed him suspiciously. 'You never did intend asking Sophie to marry you, did you?'

'No.'

Just as she'd thought! 'Then why did you say you were?'

He stood up, shrugging. 'It suited me to say so at the time.'

'You mean you lied to me!'

'Mmm, yes, it seems I did.'

Bianca was shaken by his cool confession, and the small smile playing on his lips. Had she ever really known Adam? Where would the shocks end? Still...she had to admit that he'd suddenly become a very intriguing man to be around. And very exciting.

'Will you be going back to her after this fortnight is over?' she asked, shaken by how dreadful such a prospect made her feel.

'Who knows? Maybe. It all depends.'

'On what?'

'On you, Bianca. On you.'

She stiffened when his hand snaked around her neck. He drew her slowly against him, his mouth covering hers with a confident possession which brought a moment's indignant rebellion.

But only a moment. She'd always been a sucker for aggressive lovemaking from men she wanted. Her lips parted beneath his as her pulse-rate kicked into overdrive.

Yet, strangely, his kiss gradually grew gentler, and the soft sipping at her lips brought a sweet yearning to her soul which had her clinging to him and wanting him to just go on holding her and kissing her like that. There was no urgency for more. It was just him and her, together, in each other's arms, loving each other with great tenderness. Bianca had never felt anything like it. It was just so beautiful.

'Adam,' she whispered shakily when his mouth finally lifted.

'Mmm?'

'I... I...'

She stopped herself just in time from saying the silliest things. Lord, she really had to stop mistaking these warm, squishy feelings she was feeling for love. It was just another side to sex, she supposed, a softer side which she hadn't explored as yet.

Adam—especially this new Adam—would laugh if she started telling him she loved him, or promising she would always be there for him. She almost laughed at herself. Silly Bianca. As if she could ever promise a man that anyway.

'Bianca? What were you going to say?'

She ignored the sudden stab of dismay in her heart and smiled brightly into his suddenly watchful grey eyes.

'I was just going to ask if Mum and I could come to the races with you today?'

CHAPTER EIGHT

'OH, NO I couldn't possibly do something as energetic as go to the races today,' May said when she finally surfaced around ten. 'I'm wrecked. But you two go. No, I insist,' she went on when Bianca started to object to that idea. 'I'll be fine here on my own. I'll loll around watching TV, and then I'll have a nap after lunch. What time do you think you'll be home?'

'The last race is at four-thirty,' Adam said, 'but I always leave before that. I'd say six should safely see us back. Would you like to go out for dinner tonight, May?'

'Not tonight, thank you, Adam. But I'll tell you what I would like...'

'Your wish is my command.'

'Some Chinese takeaway. No particular dish. I like just about everything Chinese.'

'Done! We'll bring a selection home with us.'

May smiled at him. 'That would be lovely.'

Adam felt quite pleased at this outcome, though actually he'd had no intention of going to the races that day at all before Bianca had asked about his coming home last night. The previous Saturday's results had taught him to give his system a rest for a while. It only worked well with top-class horses, it seemed, and they were all out on spells after the recent conclusion of the spring racing carnival, both in Melbourne and Sydney.

But he rather fancied taking Bianca to the races, he thought as he got dressed. He often saw well-heeled businessmen there on a Saturday afternoon, with their latest dolly-birds on their arms. Most of them mistresses, no doubt. They just didn't have that wifely look about their model figures and perfectly painted faces.

He'd imagined Bianca as his mistress more than once in his darker moments. He'd fantasised about becoming filthy rich and buying her for himself with the sheer power of his millions. Her lack of desire for him hadn't mattered in that scenario. She would do whatever he wanted because he was paying her exorbitant amounts of money, dressing her in designer clothes and giving her lavishly expensive gifts of jewellery.

Unfortunately, in reality Bianca was not too impressed with money, or designer clothes, or jewellery. The girl went around most of the time in shorts or jeans, her only jewellery a clunky black sports watch with which she could time her jogging. She had two androgynous-looking suits she wore to work—navy and black—mixed and matched with various cheap blouses and T-shirts. It was no wonder he had been startled to see her in something soft and feminine last night.

Still, the present pretend situation allowed him some leeway when it came to buying her things, and he didn't have to buy her desire now. He already had that. Amazingly.

This thought brought with it an elation and a boldness which, quite frankly, he was having difficulty in controlling. There wasn't anything he wouldn't dare to do. There wasn't anything he could *not* do, he decided as he pulled on a shirt.

Except win her love, came that sly voice, and he stopped buttoning his shirt for a moment, a scowl sweeping his face.

For a moment, this morning, he could have sworn Bianca had been going to tell him she loved him. He'd thought she'd felt the magic between them. But the magic had only been on his side, obviously.

All she wants from you is sex, that rotten voice went on. You'll go the same way as all the others eventually. Tossed in the garbage like a used tissue.

Adam straightened, scowling some more.

'I will not listen to you today,' he muttered to himself. 'You're destructive. And depressing. I'm happy this morning, dammit. Just shut up.'

'Talking to yourself, Adam?'

Adam whirled, his expression wryly amused when he saw that Bianca had dressed in her usual weekend garb of jeans and sleeveless T-shirt. Since he himself always wore jeans to the races—hell, he was usually there to work at winning money, not a fashion-on-the-field award—he could understand her mistake. But that was not how they were going to arrive at Randwick today.

'Just making a deal with the devil, darling,' he told her, and her eyebrows lifted.

'So that's how you win at the races, is it? By the way, Mum thinks it's rather odd that all my clothes are in the spare room, but I told her you had so much musty old junk in your wardrobe there wasn't room for mine. Now, why in heaven's name are you smiling at me like that? Is there something wrong with the way I look? *You're* only wearing jeans!'

'Too true. But I keep my racing clothes elsewhere. I'm going to change on the way, and you, my dear wife, will be changing with me.'

He was delighted to see she was totally flummoxed at this announcement. He was also delighted that the presence of her mother in the flat precluded Bianca launching into an Aussie version of the Spanish inquisition.

But peace only lasted till he bundled her into the BMW around eleven. No sooner had he pointed the car south, in the direction of the city, than she started.

'Adam, I don't like it when you keep secrets from me. I want to know—'

'Why aren't you playing netball this afternoon?' he broke in, determined not to satisfy her very female curiosity.

Her sigh was heavy. 'If you'd been around lately, you'd know I played the finals of the netball season two months ago! And my team happened to win.

Haven't you seen the trophy on top of the television?' she asked in a miffed tone.

The place was full of sports trophies Bianca had won. He was proud of her achievements, but jealous at the same time. He would rather she played with *him* than a silly old netball.

'Congratulations,' he said drily. 'But that doesn't answer my question. Isn't there a summer season?'

'Yes, but it's played at night because of the heat. I don't like playing sport at night. Night-time is for other things.'

'I'm sorry I asked,' he muttered, though not sorry she wasn't playing netball. He had other plans for Bianca this afternoon.

'Adam, you still haven't explained what you meant when you said we were going to change clothes on the way to the races. That is what you said, isn't it?'

'Yes. Tell me, Bianca, do you ever regret not doing a degree in Physical Education, as you always planned to do?'

She frowned her frustration at his changing the subject again. 'No,' she grumped, and folded her arms, obviously giving up on getting answers to her questions.

Adam smiled. Bianca not getting her own way with him had an undeniable appeal. He didn't think he would ever get tired of it.

'You don't miss being a sports mistress?' he asked, before realising what he'd said. 'Sports mistress' rather described her to a tee.

'I was very happy doing a business degree, thank you very much,' she retorted. 'If you remember rightly, there was no scholarship I could win for PE like I managed with business. Dad was dead by then and Mum was just making ends meet. A scholarship *plus* my part-time job at Franklins meant she didn't have to spend every cent on my education and she had a bit left over for luxuries for herself for a change.'

Adam sighed to himself. Just when he started thinking Bianca was a selfish chit he came face to face with her good qualities. She did so love her mother. And she wasn't at all mean and selfish when it came to material things. To be honest, she was a good friend too. When she'd said she would have pretended to be his *wife*, if he'd asked her, she'd been quite sincere. She would have. Without giving it a second thought.

'I was disappointed at first,' Bianca admitted, warming to the conversation. 'But I soon realised it didn't really matter what degree I did. I could still indulge my passion for sport in my spare time. And uni life was fantastic! I've never had such a good time as I had during those three years. It was such fun, Adam, wasn't it?'

Fun! Adam scoffed silently. That was the bottom line where Bianca was concerned. Fun! Well, *he* was going to have fun this afternoon, and he just couldn't wait!

'Indeed it was,' he agreed suavely, hiding his wicked intentions behind a wolf-like smile. 'And we're going to have more fun this afternoon. Trust me.'

Bianca fell into a blinking, wide-eyed silence while Adam simply kept smiling, neither speaking till they arrived at North Sydney and he swung off the road, driving down a ramp into the underground car park of the high-rise building which housed the penthouse unit he owned.

'I hope you're finally going to tell me what on earth we're doing here?' she demanded to know, her silence quickly giving way to angry exasperation. 'Unless Randwick Race Course has been dramatically picked up and moved indoors, I don't think we're at the races yet. Or is this the mysterious place where you keep your racing clothes?' she asked tartly. 'In a basement car park?'

'Did anyone ever tell you, Bianca,' he said smilingly as they both climbed out, 'that you're beautiful when you're mad?'

She rolled her eyes at him over the roof of the car and he laughed.

'Come on,' he said, and walked round to take her hand. 'We haven't got a lot of time.'

'For *what?*'

'For getting My Fair Lady ready for the races!' he pronounced, and, totally ignoring the bewilderment on her face, he started dragging her towards the basement lift.

The next hour was one of the best in Adam's life.

The building above them was not just an apartment block; it housed offices on the first few floors, with the ground floor being devoted to shops of all kinds. Most of these shops catered to the wealthy yuppy career woman, who possibly lived in the building or worked there.

Adam headed for the most expensive and largest boutique, which had a make-up and hairdressing section attached, told one of the superbly groomed sales-ladies what he wanted done with Bianca—amazing how helpful the woman became when he slipped her a hundred-dollar bonus for herself—then left a still stunned Bianca in her undoubtedly capable hands while he dashed upstairs to change into his grey silk-blend Italian suit.

He returned just in time to see a strikingly made-up Bianca emerge from one of the dressing rooms, hair sleekly up.

She did a double-take when she saw him standing there in his suit, but after a couple of frozen seconds she shrugged acceptance of the craziness of it all and started to parade herself for his inspection and approval.

The cream trouser suit she was wearing was elegant, but not at all what he'd had in mind.

'Well, Adam, darling?' she said in a breathy voice as she catwalked her way around the heavily mirrored display area. Wickedly laughing blue eyes showed him she'd decided to join in the spirit of the dressing-up game. 'What do you think?'

He cocked his head on one side, looked her up and down, then coolly shook his head. 'No. Cream doesn't suit you.'

She pouted prettily and gave the sales-lady a mock desolate look. 'My husband doesn't think cream suits me. Oh, dearie me, whatever will we do? Off with the cream and on with the new,' she tossed back airily as she sashayed off to the dressing room.

Adam smiled to himself. What a wicked little minx she was! But what a woman! It was no wonder he loved her. No other female he'd ever met compared with Bianca.

She came back five minutes later in a slender red silk dress with a Chinese collar and slits up the sides. She looked exotic and pretty, yet oddly innocent, almost childlike as she paraded around in her bare feet, beaming at him. Clearly she liked herself in this dress, but it was not the look he wanted.

He shook his head again. 'Very nice, but I'd like to see her in black,' he ordered. 'Something short and tight. And some high heels, please. Black, with an ankle strap.' He'd noted they had a pair like that in the small range of expensive and very sexy shoes on display in one corner of the shop.

Bianca's blue eyes opened wide for a second, as did her scarlet-glossed lips. Her mouth snapped shut at the same moment her eyes narrowed. Now she didn't look quite so happy to play this game. Her lips pouted further, as they did when she was displeased. She looked petulant, and so damned

sexy he almost changed his mind about the races.
The penthouse awaited upstairs, as did the king-
sized bed ...

But, no ... He had another fantasy in mind for
the penthouse. Today was mistress day.

Besides, tonight would eventually come. And it
would be all the better for the waiting.

It was ten minutes before she returned from the
dressing room, by which time he was dangling on
a delicious razor's edge of sexual tension, the like
of which he'd never known before. The sight of her
quite took his breath away.

The outfit was black, as ordered. A scandalously
short, tightly fitting, figure-hugging dress, with a
low, wide square neckline that barely covered her
nipples.

Adam eventually dragged his eyes away from
Bianca's tiny but well-defined breasts to travel
slowly downwards, past the expanse of bare tanned
thighs, past slender knees and beautifully shaped
calves to her erotically clad feet. The outrageously
high heels lent her legs the illusion of great length,
the sight of the ankle straps giving his desire for
her a piquant push.

He had never seen her looking sexier. Or *less*
innocent.

For a moment he imagined all the men at the
races looking at her and wanting her, and was torn
between wanting to hide her away for his eyes only
and flaunting her for all the world to see. Something dark inside him tempted to show her off, to

show everyone that at last she was *his*...even if it was only in the most elemental way.

Yes, that was what he wanted, he decided with a devilish satisfaction. There would be no hiding her body away from ogling eyes, no conventional good-guy path.

His conscience pricked a warning, but he would have none of it. This was what she wanted him to be, wasn't it? This was what turned her on. Primitive man. The predator. The possessor.

But then she looked at him and he saw a flicker of dismay in her eyes.

His instant remorse annoyed him. But it was too late. His love for Bianca resurfaced with a vengeance—as did his conscience—and he knew he would not enjoy himself if Bianca was feeling that uncomfortable.

'No, I don't think so,' he said almost regretfully. 'Not for the races. The red silk was better. But I will take the black as well,' he told the sales-lady in a husky aside. He just might have Bianca wear it for him one evening next week in the penthouse. They could have a private candlelit dinner together. Then afterwards...

'Would your...er...*wife*...like some jewellery to go with her dresses?' the sales-lady asked.

Adam was taken aback for a second by the knowing way the woman had said the word 'wife'. Clearly she didn't believe Bianca was any such thing. He gave the woman an icy glare but she wasn't fazed.

'We have some exquisite costume jewellery here,' she went on, indicating a showcase filled with dazzling pieces. 'What about these lovely black crystal drop earrings and matching bracelet? They could only enhance madam's striking beauty, don't you think?'

He did think. But when Bianca returned, wearing not only the red silk dress but the strappy black high heels, he had a moment's doubt. Once the glamorous earrings and bracelet were in place, his doubts grew. Suddenly she looked a lot less innocent than she had earlier.

Not that Bianca seemed concerned any more, he noted wryly. Her blue eyes were bright and shining with a return to her earlier mischievous manner. Why should he worry if she wasn't?

'I had no idea you had such beautiful taste in clothes, darling,' she cooed as she slipped her arm through his. 'I must have you take me shopping more often.'

Adam gave her a droll look while he silently called himself every kind of fool. He should have made her wear the black. It would have matched her devil's soul. There he'd been, thinking she was upset at being dressed up like a sex object. Instead, she was enjoying every perverse moment!

'Any time, darling,' he drawled. 'I don't mind what I spend on you as long as I get value for money.' He looked her up and down with lazy eyes, lingering on the outline of her braless nipples under the thin red silk. 'And there's no doubt you look the part perfectly.'

By the time his gaze returned to her face, Bianca's blue eyes were flashing, the high colour in her cheeks showing that her blood was rising again.

Good, he thought. Bianca in a temper was an incredibly passionate creature. She'd been spitting mad with him last night and look where it had got him. In bed with her. If he could not have her love then he'd settle for her body.

His smile was darkly triumphant as he turned her round and patted her on the backside. 'Now off you go and collect your old clothes, darling,' he said thickly, 'while I pay for your nice new ones.'

All together, counting the dresses, shoes and jewellery, the bill came to a little over three thousand dollars—not counting the tip he'd given the woman. Still, in Adam's view it had been worth every cent. This was going to be a fun afternoon after all!

He paid with his bankcard, knowing that what he'd won at the casino this week covered it more than twice over. He could have paid cash, but he wanted to keep that for the races. He was going to bet big this afternoon, in keeping with the occasion. He'd never been on such a dangerous high before. Never felt this bold, or this deliciously bad.

Adam was sure that if he could keep his stupid conscience out of play, he was really going to enjoy himself.

*   *   *

Bianca could not stop staring at Adam as he led her back towards the bank of lifts which would carry them down to the basement car park. Partly because he looked incredibly handsome—wherever had that gorgeous grey suit come from?—but mostly because of the expression on his face. There was something dark and dangerous lurking in his cold, yet strangely *hot* grey eyes. Something...wicked.

Adam being wicked held a kind of shocked fascination—especially since Bianca had spent her entire life thinking of him as a bit of a goody-two-shoes. Clearly he was far from that.

Still, his being wicked could be fun. She'd actually enjoyed herself back in the boutique, had revelled in the whole dressing-up game. Yet the finished result was a far cry from the classily dressed My Fair Lady, off to Royal Ascot. She looked more like Suzie Wong, ready for a night on the town. If her mother could have seen her, she'd have had a pink fit! She'd certainly be asking her daughter some pertinent questions.

Bianca herself was determined not to let Adam keep sidestepping her own questions.

'Mind telling me what's going on, darling?' she asked saucily as they waited for the lift doors to open. 'Do you make a habit of tarting up your female friends for an afternoon at the races? Or is this charade just for me, for some reason?'

His smile was irritatingly sardonic. 'Now don't be tedious and start asking more useless questions. I have no intention of answering them.'

Which was another thing that was bothering her. This increasingly enigmatic and uncooperative side of Adam's character. She'd been so right when she'd thought him a stranger before. He was.

'The least you can do is tell me where you got your suit from?'

'Why?'

'Because I want to know! Did you rent it? Yes, I'll bet you did. Like you rented that tux you were wearing last night. There's a clothes rental shop in this building, isn't there?'

The lift doors opened and he walked in, turning to smile at her from the far corner. 'Just get in, Bianca.'

Pursing her lips together, she tried to stalk in with her usual long stride, only to wobble on the appallingly high heels she was wearing. 'Watch it,' he said, reaching out to steady her.

She wrenched her arm away and glared her temper at him. 'If I wasn't wearing these tart's shoes, I'd be fine.'

'I didn't ask you to wear them. Not with the red silk, anyway,' he added drily.

'I could hardly wear my old trainers. Or nothing at all!'

'No, nothing at all would not have been suitable.'

'Neither was that disgusting black dress I was poured into—the one you still bought.' She rattled the large plastic shopping bag at him, which contained her old clothes plus the black bit of nothing. 'If you think I'd ever wear that whore's dress in public, then you have another think coming!'

'I have no intention of letting you wear that particular number in public, Bianca. It's for my eyes only.'

She blinked widely at him as an image of her parading around in private for him in the black mini popped into her mind. She'd exaggerated when she'd called it a whore's dress. It wasn't *that* bad. A lot of girls dressed like that these days when going out at night. Short, tight and sexy was in. But she'd never felt comfortable displaying her lack of any real cleavage.

Still, she had to admit that when Adam had looked at her in that dress, she'd been...well, she'd been very turned on. She had been quite discomfited by the fact, especially when she'd felt her breasts swell and her nipples tighten.

In truth, she *still* felt turned on. She only had G-string panties on, which had been fine under jeans but made her feel half-naked and very sensuous underneath a thin silk dress. She didn't even have any tights for security, and was very aware of her bare thighs and buttocks. On top of that, her nipples had stayed erect, poking like little pebbles against the cool red silk.

'I still feel decidedly undressed,' she complained.

'Is it my fault you don't wear a bra?'

'You don't want me wearing a bra and you know it,' she countered sharply. 'I'm not dumb, Adam. I finally get the picture. This is the price I have to pay for you pretending to be my husband, isn't it? I not only have to take over Sophie's duties in bed but everywhere else as well! I saw the way she was dressed the other night. You have this *thing* for tarted up women, don't you?'

Once again he said nothing, just leant his back against the far wall of the lift and surveyed her slowly, his eyes darkening as they moved inexorably to her nipples.

'You look incredible,' he said in a desire-thickened voice.

'I look cheap,' she snapped.

He laughed. 'Hardly cheap. That outfit set me back a pretty penny.'

'And that's another thing,' she said, frowning. 'I know what it means when dresses don't have price-tags on them. It's the same as restaurants which don't have prices on the menus. It means everything's horribly expensive. You're not that rich, Adam, that you can afford to throw your money around like confetti. You shouldn't be wasting your hard-earned money like this.'

The lift doors opened and Adam levered himself away from the wall. 'Don't you worry your pretty little head about what I spend my money on, Bianca. You're not my *real* wife.

'Now...' He took her arm and began leading her forcefully across the car park 'Let's get moving. By the time we get to Randwick we'll have missed the first race. But no matter—the first couple of races are never the best ones to bet on.'

Bianca thought of standing her ground and *demanding* some answers, but, in truth, she suspected Adam would be as good as his word. He wasn't going to tell her where his own expensive clothes had come from, or deny or confirm why he'd had her dolled up like some sex-pot.

Besides, she had to admit that beneath her exasperation lay an excitement which would not be denied. It *was* fun to be dolled up like this, and to have her blood zinging through her veins. She felt not a little wicked herself, so when she climbed into the passenger seat and the slits in her dress parted, exposing most of her stockingless thighs, she made no attempt to cover herself. She might not have big boobs, but she had great legs!

Adam likes to see female flesh, she thought breathlessly. Then female flesh he will see!

When Adam glared down at her expanse of exposed thigh with disapproval on his face, Bianca was thrown completely. Wasn't this the sort of thing that turned him on? Apparently not . . . if his scowl was anything to go by.

'I think, darling wife,' he muttered as he fired the engine, 'that we'll be standing up all afternoon.'

Bianca could only shake her head in utter bewilderment when Adam reversed rather angrily out of the parking space. Now she had no idea what game he was playing. Or what he felt for her. Or what role he expected her to fulfil this afternoon.

He'd become a mystery man, all right. But a rather fascinating man as well, she realised as she slid a sideways glance over at his closed but very handsome face. Her gaze drifted down to his lips, which at that moment were pressed testily together. His full bottom lip was jutting forward a little. It looked incredibly sexy. *He* looked incredibly sexy.

Desire knotted her stomach and she thought, all of a sudden, of the many hours which separated her from going to bed with Adam tonight.

Too many, she decided ruefully as she felt the blood begin to gallop around her veins. Far too many...

By the time Bianca uncurled herself from the passenger seat of the BMW half an hour later, she had her wayward body only partially under control. Standing up, she skimmed the red silk dress back down her thighs in an unconsciously nervous movement, at the same time trying not to wobble in her five-inch heels.

Adam watched her with another of those unnervingly sardonic smiles he'd suddenly discovered. He was no longer looking disapproving of how she looked. Just drily amused.

Rebellion surfaced along with her ongoing frustration.

He wanted a sexual exhibit on his arm? Well, he'd get one. And to hell with the consequences!

CHAPTER NINE

ADAM wasn't enjoying himself as much as he'd thought he would. The next bloke who leered at Bianca was going to get a fist in his face!

Of course, *she* was having the time of her life, the lying little devil. There she'd been, pretending she didn't like the way she looked, but since she'd started being on the receiving end of ogling male eyes, she'd been lapping it all up like a cat with cream.

She'd sashayed her way around the course, fluttering her eyelashes at every man they passed and wiggling that sexy bottom of hers, which was looking *so* sexy in that red dress it was downright sinful.

On top of that, she'd already downed more glasses of champagne than he'd ever seen a female down and stay standing. No doubt she was as high as a kite, because she'd started to giggle—something Bianca never did—and to drape herself all over him—something else Bianca never, *ever* did, not with any man.

By the fourth race Adam had just about had enough. He wanted to leave, but, darn it all, he was winning again, weirdly enough. A punter never left the track when he was winning, though the next race left a lot to be desired.

'Oh, look, the darling horseys are coming out!' Bianca explained, with the best bimbo vocabulary Adam had ever heard. 'Which one are you going to put your money on, honey?' she gushed, holding onto his arm so tightly Adam suspected it was to keep her upright, not because she was inordinately fond of him.

'I wish I knew,' he said drily. 'The next race is a two-thousand-metre event which doesn't have a single runner tried at the distance. I'll just have to try pot luck with a combination on top trainer and top jockey.'

'Why don't you use that wonderful old system you foisted on us unsuspecting students during our first year at university?' Bianca suggested with a saucy smile. 'You know, the one where you were going to turn our miserable hundred dollars each into a fortune? It didn't do too badly, I suppose,' she went on, her blue eyes glittering with wicked amusement. 'Only twenty-nine consecutive losers!'

Adam cringed at the memory. What a fiasco! 'Trust you to remind me. Still, I've learnt a thing or two about racehorse systems since then. *And* staking plans. You need a damn sight more than a few hundred dollars to start with if you wish to survive!'

'I'll bet I could pick you the winner,' she said, with the blithe confidence of the merrily intoxicated. 'If it's a long race and none of them have

run with distance before then the fittest will undoubtedly win. I'm an expert on fitness. Come
on...'

She dragged him over to the railing on the sad-
dling enclosure, where the horses were still being
led around in circles by their grooms.

'Look at that one!' she pointed out eagerly. 'Talk
about rippling muscles. Have you ever seen a fantastic rump like that one?'

'Er...' Adam gave Bianca's own well-defined
rump a rueful glance. 'Not too often.'

'That's definitely the winner!' Bianca announced, after another minute's superficial survey.
'There's not another horse to touch it. I demand
you put a bet on that one for me.'

'All right. If you insist.' She'd die when she saw
the ticket, but it would be sweet vengeance for her
amusing herself at his expense.

Smiling, he propped a sozzled Bianca up against
the railing, then went to place the bet at the tote
window before hurrying back. He had a feeling he
didn't dare leave Bianca alone for long. She looked
far too delicious. And she was far too tipsy.

He'd been right. By the time he returned, less
than five minutes later, some good-looking
slimeball with a moustache and money written all
over him was chatting her up. Bianca was looking
up at him with a rapt expression, as though he were
God's personal messenger, and it took all of
Adam's control not to walk up and thump the creep
right in his perfectly capped teeth.

As it was, his voice was glacial as he joined them and said, 'Thanks so much for looking after my wife. But I'll take her back now.' And, clamping an iron grip around Bianca's upper arm, he practically dragged her off, not stopping till he found a relatively secluded corner.

'Ooh, how masterful!' Bianca said, then giggled.

'You're plastered,' he snapped, whirling her round to face him.

'You noticed!'

'And you're acting like a cheap whore.'

'Well, of course! Isn't that what you wanted?'

Her words hit him like a low blow in the stomach.

No, of course that was not what he wanted. He wanted her as his wife, not his whore.

Still, he couldn't deny she'd so aroused him that afternoon that he could not stand another moment's torture.

'Let's get out of here,' he said brusquely.

Her lovely but slightly glazed eyes blinked up at him. 'But you just put a bet on that horsey for me.'

'It's collectable any time if it wins,' he growled, and, taking her elbow, began to steer her back through the crowd.

'Where...where are you taking me?'

'Somewhere we can be alone.'

She ground to a halt, swaying on her high heels as she did so. 'I never thought you were the type of man to take advantage of a girl,' she said, her voice slurring.

He laughed. 'Your mistake, then.' And to prove his point he bent to take her startled mouth in a brief, hungry kiss. When his head lifted her eyes were glazed in a way which suggested he could take advantage of her all he liked and she would not object. The thought sent his conscience to hell, and he aimed to keep it there.

This was the life! For the time being, anyway. He was under no illusions that it would last. He figured he would at least have the next fortnight with her, maybe even a month to two . . . if he could keep up the bad-boy act long enough and well enough.

But sooner or later his masquerade would be discovered, and Bianca would see that underneath he was the same old Adam he'd always been. Once that happened this spark he'd managed to fire in her would no doubt be snuffed out, and she would cut him adrift again.

A black despair invaded his heart at this inevitability, and it was with some difficulty that he blocked it from his mind. He managed quite well once he turned his thoughts to taking advantage of her in the very near future.

'No more chit-chat,' he snapped, and resumed propelling his torment back to the car.

Irritatingly, she did what he asked, not saying a single word during the drive back from Randwick to North Sydney. Her silence grated on his nerves, and he began to worry about what she would say when she saw the penthouse. Not that he intended telling her all. Bad boys never explained, or confided. They simply shrugged off questions then took what they wanted.

'What are we doing back here?' Bianca was finally driven to ask when he directed the BMW into the same basement car park he'd taken her to that morning. 'Do you have to bring your suit back? Is that it?'

Adam frowned his puzzlement. 'What in God's name are you talking about, Bianca? I own this suit.'

'Oh. I . . . I thought you must have rented it.'

'Your mistake again. Stay there,' he said as he switched off the engine. 'I'll come round and help you out.'

Which he did—not so much to act the gentleman, but to leer nicely at her naked legs, the sight of which had tormented him all afternoon. Looking at her firm brown thighs did little, however, for his resolve not to rush things once he got her upstairs.

'Where are you taking me?' she asked shakily as he led her once again to the bank of lifts.

'Somewhere private.'

'Must you be so mysterious?' she threw at him once they were in the lift.

'It saves answering a whole lot of unnecessary questions.' And unnecessary arguments. He'd brought her here for sex, dammit, not for true confessions.

He should have known that wouldn't be the end of it. When he inserted the key into the lift lock

for the top floor, she started up again. 'You're
taking me up to an apartment, aren't you? This
building is one of those where they've converted
the upper floors for city living. Who owns it? A
friend of yours? The university?'

'Let's just say I have access to it,' he bit out.
'Now why don't you put a lid on it, Bianca? You're
driving me crazy with all your questions. I haven't
brought you here to cross-examine me.'

The lift jolted a little as it began its upward ride,
and tipsy Bianca rocked against Adam's chest. His
arms shot around her, one large palm landing on
her bottom. His eyes locked with hers while slowly
he pleated the red silk upwards till his fingertips
encountered a delicious expanse of pouting and
shockingly bare buttock.

Bianca's eyes turned a smoky blue at this point.
Her lips fell apart and her tongue-tip moved se-
ductively between her teeth in a tormentingly erotic
way.

'I'm beginning to realise that,' she whispered, in
the sort of voice which would have aroused a
zombie. 'Perhaps you'd better show me exactly
what you had in mind...'

'That was the best Chinese food I've had in years!'
May pronounced, leaning back in her chair with a
big smile on her face. 'But I've eaten way too much.
You shouldn't have bought so many dishes, Adam.
I've made a right little piggie of myself.'

'Nonsense! Chinese food's like that. In half an hour you'll be wanting to eat something else. Another glass of wine?'

'Just half a glass.'

'What about you, Bianca?'

'No, no more wine.' She placed her hand over her glass, but could not bring herself to look at him.

She'd sobered up considerably since their torrid lovemaking session that afternoon. My God, she had never known anything like it. It had been really wild.

Somehow they had made it inside the penthouse apartment before Adam had shown her well and truly why he'd brought her there. Not that she'd minded his savage haste. She'd been wanting him all afternoon, had been dying for his touch and his body. Neither of them had been able to wait, ravaging each other up against the door without turning on the light. They hadn't even undressed properly.

But that hadn't been the end of it. Adam had then carried her temporarily satisfied body to the biggest bed she'd ever seen, where he'd proceeded to drive her crazy for ages on what had seemed like acres of blue satin sheets. She had never realised any man could know so much about a woman's body, or how to torment it for so long without release. He had dangled her on a bittersweet edge till she'd been moaning and groaning. And begging. Dear heaven, how she'd begged!

But it hadn't been the begging that had bothered her. In a way that had been exciting. For she had known, in her heart, that Adam had not been trying to punish her. He'd been making her pleasure last. When she'd finally gone over the edge, it had been incredible.

It had been her thoughts afterwards which had upset her. And the inevitable conclusions she'd come to once she'd really taken in her surroundings.

She'd been lying there on those satin sheets, exhausted, glancing around the spacious bedroom with its mirrored wardrobes and plate glass windows and stunning view of the harbour, when she realised that this could not be the first time Adam had used this orgy palace for assignations with the opposite sex. The certainty that he had brought that ghastly Sophie there, had had sex with her in that very bed, had turned her stomach.

She just hadn't been able to lie there after that, and had scrambled out of the bed and dashed for the shower, calling out to Adam that it was late and would he please get her own clothes from the car. She'd bundled up the other clothes, which had been scattered around the place, stuffed them in the shopping bag, along with the jewellery, and left them there.

If he had noticed her change of mood he hadn't said anything—highlighting, to her, the fact that he didn't give a damn about her feelings. All he'd wanted from her was sex. The truth was that he'd dolled her up like a whore that morning and then treated her like a whore. Even worse, she'd *acted* like a whore.

She'd been relieved to leave that hateful place behind, plus those hateful clothes. She hoped Adam thought they were worth the money he'd paid for them. Maybe he could dress up his next bed partner in them! The surety that there would be other silly girls who would do what he wanted in the future was depressing in the extreme.

'You're very quiet, Bianca,' her mother said. 'And you haven't eaten much either. Aren't you feeling well?'

With an effort, she found a small smile. 'I have a bad headache,' she said. Which she did. Champagne did it to her every time, once the initial effect wore off.

'You look tired too, darling,' her mother went on. 'Why don't you go to bed early tonight?'

'I think I will.' She stood up and started clearing the plates away. At least when she was asleep she couldn't think, or feel upset.

'Adam and I'll do that,' May said. 'You go pop in the shower and get into bed. Would you like me to make you a cup of cocoa?'

'No, thanks, Mum. I'll be fine.'

But she wasn't fine. She crawled into bed feeling utterly wretched. Everything was so mixed up in her head. She tried telling herself that she couldn't possibly be in love with this new Adam, that beneath his sexy exterior he was quite hateful, really, nothing at all like the nice, kind, sweet person she'd grown up with—the one she'd always believed really cared about her.

This Adam didn't care about her. And he wasn't at all nice—no matter how well he was fooling her mother out there. He was hard and ruthless and selfish.

What had changed him? Had he been changing all along and she just hadn't noticed?

She lay there for what felt like hours, her head pounding, her heart just as bad. She must really love him to feel this badly. Just a sexual attraction couldn't possibly cause this much misery.

But he didn't love her back. He really didn't. He was amusing himself with her. And using her.

Dismay soon turned to outrage. She wasn't going to let him use her again. Or touch her again. Just let him try!

When he finally came into the room to go to bed, she lay perfectly still under the bedclothes, glad she'd found a big T-shirt of his to wear to bed. It came right down past her knees—knees which were bent right up to her chest. She was curled up in a foetal position, her eyes tightly shut, her back turned towards his side of the bed.

She listened to the sound of the shower, then to the sounds of his coming back into the room. She froze further when she felt the quilt lift, then flinched at the feel of his body settling behind hers.

For an excruciatingly long moment she thought she was safe. But then he took her shoulder and rolled her over against his naked side. 'No,' she said on a strangled sob of despair. For even that small contact made her want to melt against him. 'I . . . I still have a headache.'

'I doubt that. Care to tell me what's really bugging you, Bianca? I'm not a fool. You've been in a mood since before we left North Sydney.'

'I . . . I don't want you to touch me any more.'

'Really?' There was ice in his voice. 'What's brought about this change of attitude? You sure as hell didn't mind my touching you this afternoon. In fact, you couldn't get enough.'

'I was drunk.'

'Maybe, but you weren't drunk last night, sweetheart, and you were just as accommodating then. Don't give me this garbage. Tell me the truth.'

'Very well. I don't like being used!'

'Used?'

'Yes, used,' she snapped, scornful of his attempt to sound shocked. 'I'm sure you're familiar with the concept.'

He actually laughed.

Bianca was mortified. 'How dare you laugh at me?' she snarled. 'You're nothing but an unconscionable, hard-hearted, cold-blooded, ruthless rake, and I hate you!'

'Oh, no, you don't,' he returned, still chuckling drily. 'You probably think you're in love with me. God, but it's ironic. But don't worry. You'll soon be yourself again, darling. Being in love is only a temporary passion with you. So I'm going to keep on touching you, *and* making love to you. Let me burn out your unwanted fires that way, Bianca. It's much more fun.'

'Fun! Is that all you can think of these days? Fun?'

'Yep. I was taught by an expert. Now stop this nonsense and let me get on with restoking your flames. Methinks they've temporarily gone out.' He dropped light, teasing kisses on her outraged mouth till she simply didn't have the will to argue.

'You're incorrigible,' she muttered.

'And you're beautiful.'

She stiffened as his hand started stroking softly up and down her thigh. 'You have no conscience at all, do you?' she groaned. 'And you're still using me.' She trembled when that tantalising hand travelled higher. 'Men are all the same when it comes to sex.'

'Do you want me to stop?'

She sucked in a sharp breath as that hand found its mark. 'If you do,' she whispered breathlessly, 'I'll kill you.'

CHAPTER TEN

THE sun was shining brightly when Bianca slowly surfaced the following morning. Adam was sitting up in bed beside her, reading the Sunday papers and looking for all the world as if he'd been doing the same thing every Sunday for years.

His hair was tousled and there was stubble on his chin. But he looked utterly gorgeous, she thought, a wave of weakness flooding through her.

Oh, well. She acknowledged with wry acceptance her own ongoing susceptibility for this man. She'd never been renowned for her ability to resist gorgeous men!

He beamed over at her as she yawned and stretched. 'Guess what?' he said brightly. 'It won. That nag you made me bet on before we left the races yesterday. Better still, it was twenty to one! What say we go buy you a new car today?'

'Don't be silly,' she said, yawning again. 'One little bet isn't going to buy me a new car. Not unless you put a couple of thousand dollars on it.'

'Sorry. I only put one.'

'One dollar. Gee whiz. What are you planning on buying me with that? A toy car?'

'Nope. I thought a brand new Nissan Sports would suit you. With a red stripe down the side. Come on, let's go.'

'*What?*' She sat bolt-upright before she remembered she was naked. 'You've gone mad, haven't you?' she pronounced agitatedly as she snatched the sheet up over her breasts. 'Or you're on drugs. Is that it? You've been taking something?'

'The only thing I'm hooked on is you, darling,' he returned, and leant over to plant a kiss on her gaping mouth. 'Can't have my best girl driving her mum around in a dangerous, rusted old rattle-trap, can I?'

Bianca was shaking her head. 'Now I know you *are* mad. I don't feel I can take advantage of someone who's gone temporarily insane.'

'Why not? I am.' With this cryptic comment, he climbed out of bed and carried his beautiful body towards the bathroom. 'Come on, Bianca. The salesmen await. It wasn't one dollar I had on that noble nag. It was one thousand.'

'One *thousand*!' Bianca squawked, leaping out of bed and chasing after him. 'What on earth are you doing, betting big sums of money like that?'

'Winning,' he replied with a cheeky grin.

'But...but you won't always win, Adam,' she pointed out in a panicky concern for him. 'Sooner or later you'll start losing. No one wins for ever.'

The smile faded on his face as he yanked her under the shower with him. 'You think I don't know that?' he growled. 'Look, I'm winning now. And it's making me bloody happy. I'll worry about losing when I start losing—fair enough?'

She stared up into his suddenly harsh eyes and wondered if she'd missed something. But then his mouth pulled back into a wicked smile and the moment was gone.

'Here,' he said, lifting up her hand and smacking a cake of soap into the palm. 'Make yourself useful, woman. I washed you last time. Now it's your turn.'

He bought her a new white Pulsar Sports with a red stripe down the side, even getting air-conditioning thrown in with the deal. Bianca was still in a bit of a daze as she followed Adam home in her lovely new car, her impressed mother by her side.

'What a lucky girl you are, Bianca, to have a man like Adam as your husband. He's so kind and generous. And he just adores the ground you walk on. There again ... he always did. Never seen a boy so besotted by a girl as he was by you during your schooldays. I always felt rather sorry for him, loving you so much, because I was afraid you'd never see his worth, or feel about him the same way he felt about you.'

Her mother's ravings rather snapped Bianca out of her appreciative daze. For what her mother didn't know was that Adam was no longer that same besotted boy. He was a man. And very different from the slave-like adolescent her mother was describing. His kindness and generosity came with a price-tag these days, she realised as she thought of those clothes he'd bought her. And now this car...

Would he expect to be repaid in kind?

Her mouth went dry at the thought.

'By the way,' her mouth was rattling on, 'I didn't like to say in front of Adam, but that Derek fellow rang yesterday while you were out. It gave me great satisfaction to tell him you were at the races with your husband. You could have cut the silence on the other end of the line with a knife,' she finished smugly.

Bianca frowned. She didn't really care whether Derek believed she was married to Adam—at least it would keep him away—but she would have to remember to click on the answering machine in future, if they ever went out again leaving her mother behind. Otherwise some silly caller might let the cat out of the bag over Adam and herself.

This thought led to another. What if someone just 'dropped in' during the next fortnight? Michelle was given to doing that occasionally. Thank God she was away up the coast, visiting her parents. It was also as well that those same parents had retired recently and moved up to said coast, far away from Sydney. Still, Adam's parents rang him most weeks. She would have to tell Adam to ring them himself, during the day, thereby heading off any awkward possibilities.

Bianca was mulling over what else she might have forgotten which would expose Adam and herself as frauds, when a small tan dog dashed across the road in front of her. Her heart leapt into her mouth as she braked and swerved, almost sideswiping another car. All to no avail. The awful clunking sound under the front wheels was sickeningly loud and unmistakable.

She'd hit the poor thing.

Her hands were shaking as she pulled over to the side of the road and turned off the engine, dreading what she would see when she climbed out. 'Stay in the car, Mum,' she ordered, sounding much more in control than she felt.

It was worse than she'd expected. Much worse.

The pathetic bundle of matted fur was lying in the gutter, his head lolling limply to one side, one of its back legs twisted at an impossible angle and a bloodied area around the hip. Bianca bent to look closer. The pup didn't have a collar round its throat and it wasn't moving.

It's dead, that's why, Bianca thought numbly as she bent to touch it lightly. I killed it. I'm a murderer.

She straightened and looked away, feeling sick. Adam, who must have seen what had happened in his rear-vision mirror and pulled over as well, came running back up the pavement.

'What happened? You almost hit that car. Dear God, Bianca, you scared me to death. For a moment there, I... Dear heaven, you're as white as a sheet. Oh, darling, don't cry,' he said, and gathered her to him. 'There, there,' he soothed, stroking her hair and cuddling her close. 'There's no need to cry. A miss is as good as a mile.'

'But I didn't miss,' she sobbed. 'I wasn't concentrating. I was thinking of my new car and...and other things, and then...and then it was just there, and I...I... Oh, Adam, I killed it!' she wailed, and buried her tearstained face in the warm expanse of his chest.

'Killed what?'

'That poor little dog,' she said, turning from his arms to point down the gutter.

It was then that the animal lifted his head and whimpered.

Bianca burst out of Adam's arms. 'It's *alive*!' She raced over and knelt down in the gutter, and patted the frightened puppy on the head. 'Oh, Adam, look, it's alive! Look, I didn't kill it.'

He *was* looking, with a wry smile on his face. 'So I see. I suppose you'll want me to take it to the vet now, and pay for all its bills, and then find it a home.'

'Well, it doesn't have a collar, Adam. And it's so skinny and scrawny. If anyone owns it, they're certainly not looking after it. But I can pay for the vet bills myself, if you'll help me get it there. I'm not that poor, and I've almost finished paying you back for my plane trip to Scotland.'

Her mother joining them at that stage rather put paid to that line of conversation. 'What's going on?' she asked. It was then that she saw the dog. 'Oh, the poor little thing.'

'Adam's going to take it to the vet, aren't you?' Bianca said, looking up at him with pleading eyes.

He squatted down beside her, his hand on her arm as gentle as his expression. 'Of course,' he said softly. 'Did you think I wouldn't?'

Tears pricked at her eyes, for underneath she'd been worried that the new Adam might have a hard heart all the way through. Now she saw that down deep there was still a soft core. He was still someone she could count on, and the sense of relief was enormous. Her gaze blurred and she leant forward to kiss him on the cheek. 'Thank you,' she whispered.

He said nothing, merely patted her on the arm.

After a few seconds he stood up. 'I've got a blanket in my boot. You stay put with the dog while I go and get it.'

'It looks like a terrier of some kind,' her mother ventured while they awaited Adam's return. 'A nice-looking little dog.'

'I'm going to keep him if he gets better,' Bianca suddenly decided, blinking hard to stop herself from crying.

'You can't keep a dog in a flat, Bianca,' her mother said, with typical Scottish practicality. 'Do be sensible.'

'Then I'll move into a house,' she said stubbornly.

'I think Adam might have something to say about that, don't you?'

'What will I have something to say about?' Adam said on rejoining them. He knelt down and began spreading a blue blanket alongside the injured animal.

May pretended not to see Bianca's warning glance. 'Your wife wants to move to a house,' she said blithely, 'so that she can keep this dog. Actually, I agree with her—not so much because of the dog, but because a flat is not the best place to raise a family, no matter how nice it is.'

Bianca's silent groan was echoed in her face, but no one was looking at her. Adam's attention was all on the dog as he rolled it gently onto the blanket and Bianca's mother was watching him for some reaction, burbling on with meddling intent.

'You know, Bianca has always held the opinion she wouldn't make a good mother, but that's not so. My daughter has a wealth of maternal instinct in her. That's why she's always lavishing love on animals. I think she'd make a marvellous mother, don't you, Adam?'

Bianca saw the flash of scepticism in Adam's eyes before he wiped them of all expression and looked up at his pretend mother-in-law. 'I'm sure you know your daughter better than anyone, May,' he said as he wrapped the dog securely in the blanket and scooped him up. 'But I suggest you don't hold your breath on becoming a grandmother. Bianca has a mind of her own, and she just doesn't see herself as a mother just yet.'

Bianca could not have agreed with Adam more. Though the conversation brought back to mind that niggling qualm about the other night, when Adam had slept with her without protection. Still, her conceiving a baby on that one-off occasion would be like a thousand to one shot winning a race. When she looked at it like that, she decided it wasn't worth worrying about. One day a period would come along. And if it didn't... well, she'd cross that bridge when she came to it.

'Mum, you're being a meddling mother-in-law,' Bianca pronounced sternly, though she did feel a little sorry for her mother.

May had wanted a big family herself, but hadn't been blessed with one. And now her only daughter wasn't going to fulfil her very natural wish to compensate by having a tribe of grandchildren. She'd be lucky if she got *one* grandchild at some time in the nebulous future.

Bianca felt rotten about it but could hardly rectify the situation. It wasn't *her* fault she was lacking in the right hormones to become a prolific breeder. Like mother, like daughter, it seemed.

'Adam, do you want us to come with you to the vet?' she asked. 'You might need someone to hold the dog while you're driving.'

'No, I don't think so. This little fellow's not going anywhere, and I can keep a good eye on him in the passenger seat. I suggest you go on home—if you feel capable of driving, that is.'

'I'll be OK. It's only a few miles from here. I'll take it slowly.'

'You do that.'

'Adam...'

'Yes?'

'Oh...nothing.' She'd been going to thank him again, but that would look a bit funny in front of her mother. 'We'll see you later.'

'I could be quite a while,' he warned.

'I'll put dinner on. Is there anything special you want?'

'You know I like anything you cook, Bianca. Now do let me get this dog to the hospital or he'll die on me, and then there'll be hell to pay!'

'You and Adam have a wonderful relationship,' May said, once mother and daughter were on their way. 'Being best friends before you became lovers was probably all for the best.'

Bianca felt a sudden urge to shock her mother out of thinking everything was perfect, Adam included. What would be her reaction, she wondered, if she learnt it was Adam who'd taken her daughter's virginity, when she was only seventeen? May had always thought Adam was such a nice, quiet, good boy. So had I, Bianca thought. Till recently.

But to reveal that old piece of history would be so unfair. That hadn't been Adam's idea.

'We still have our problems, Mum,' she said instead. 'And don't you go believing what he said about that Sophie woman. He slept with her, all right.'

'Oh, no. No, I won't accept that. Your Adam loves *you*, my girl. He was only trying to make you jealous with that flashy piece of goods, like he said.'

Bianca shook her head. Little did her mother know that Adam *liked* flashy pieces of goods in general. He'd turned *her* into a flashy piece yesterday. Her mother would have *died* if she'd seen her.

'Much the same as you were doing with that Derek person,' her mother added. 'I know you too well to believe you were unfaithful to Adam, darling. You're the most faithful girl I know, once you've decided you love someone. In the past, that love has been somewhat misguided, but I can see with Adam that you love him now as much as he loves you.'

Bianca swallowed as tears threatened again. She wished. 'I hope so, Mum. But no more talk about babies, please. I can't even *think* of babies while my marriage is on shaky ground. Having a baby would be the worst thing I could do at this moment.' Which it most certainly would!

'Your marriage, my girl, is as solid as a rock,' her mother pronounced with irritating certainty.

Bianca almost laughed. 'How can you *say* that? Two days ago my husband was dripping all over another very sexy woman.'

'I just can.'

'Second sense?'

'Common sense. And my own two eyes!'

'Whatever you say, Mum,' Bianca agreed, with a weary sigh. Thank God she was only going to be with them for a fortnight. Bianca loved her mother very much, but she loved her even more from afar!

CHAPTER ELEVEN

'It was so good of you to buy me a business class ticket back home, Adam,' May said warmly. 'You're still a good boy. Now, look after my girl for me, won't you?' And she gave him a peck on the cheek.

Adam nodded, then stood back a little while mother and daughter said their goodbyes, doing his best to watch them without depression setting in. The call had come to board the British Airways flight to Edinburgh. It was time for Bianca's mother to leave, and time for his pretend marriage to Bianca to end.

Perhaps it was all for the best, he reasoned, firmly pushing aside his emotions to concentrate on logic. How long could he have kept playing a combination of perfect husband and perfect playboy?

In May's company he'd been as nice and wholesome as apple pie, but behind closed doors he'd kept up the bad-boy act, never taking no for an answer to his demands, but never answering Bianca's own perfectly natural questions about his gambling habits, and that puzzling penthouse and what he'd been up to in it.

Yet it was the bad boy she'd fallen in love with, not good old loyal Adam.

Which left him *where*, if he wanted to keep Bianca in love with him? Being a bastard for ever? She would eventually grow bored with that as well, he knew, so what was the point?

The point, he decided, with a surge of ruthless resolve, was to keep her in his life and in his bed as long as possible. Maybe he might even marry her for real while she was vulnerable to this new side of himself. Who knew what he might do?

Adam frowned. Hell, was being a bastard becoming second nature to him?

Bianca returned to his side, red-eyed and sniffling. 'She's gone,' she croaked.

He gave her his hankie and put a comforting arm around her shoulder. 'Do you want to stay and watch the plane take off?'

'No, I hate that.' She blew her nose noisily. 'I'd rather go visit Lucky.'

Adam sighed. 'That mangy dog again. You visited him the other day, didn't you?'

'I've been visiting him *every* day. You've been happily at work, so you wouldn't know.'

Happily at work? That was a joke.

It was as well his students had been doing end-of-year exams these past two weeks, as his concentration had been shot to bits. Lecturing in maths required a clear brain and some focus, but all he'd been able to think about all day every day was getting home to Bianca. He was glad it was Saturday and he had the rest of the weekend with her.

It was only ten in the morning and the sun was shining. The rest of the day stretched ahead, warm and sensuous and theirs alone. He didn't want to waste too much of it visiting a dog, no matter how cute it was. Truly, he was beginning to feel jealous of that animal.

'You don't honestly mean to keep him, do you?' he asked.

'I certainly do. The vet said he'd be ready to go home tomorrow.'

'Might I remind you that all that talk of moving into a house was just talk for your mother.'

'I suspected as much,' she said glumly. 'But I do have friends, you know. Maybe one of them can look after Lucky for a while, till I can find a house to share with someone.'

'Such as whom?' Adam snapped. God, she meant to leave him for that damned dog! It felt as if he'd been kicked in the stomach. So much for his belief that even the bastard in him had captured her love.

She shrugged and stuffed the hankie into her jeans' back pocket. 'I don't know. I'll find someone.'

'I dare say you will,' he said sourly. Bianca had a knack for getting people to do things for her—himself included.

'Oh, all right,' he growled by the time they reached the car. 'I'll look around for a house.'

Her face was almost worth the effort he knew it would take, selling his unit and finding a house which wouldn't break his bank. Of course, if he sold the penthouse he would have plenty of money. But, damn it all, he didn't *want* to sell the penthouse. It gave him a real buzz, using the place— especially with Bianca in tow. He was planning on taking her there tonight.

'I'll go see some real estate agents today,' he added resignedly.

'Oh, Adam!' she exclaimed, and threw herself into his arms, covering his face with kisses. 'I do so love you!'

He grabbed her shoulders and held her away from him. 'Do you, Bianca?' he ground out, his heart thudding with a mixture of desire and anger. 'Do you really? This isn't just gratitude talking?'

Confusion clouded her lovely eyes for a moment. 'No,' she said at last, but in a tentative voice. 'No, it's not gratitude.'

'You love *me*?' He scowled with all the cynicism the years of rejection had put there. 'Adam Marsden? The same Adam Marsden you met in kindergarten?'

'Yes,' she said with heart-wrenching certainty, and went to kiss him again, this time on the mouth.

He stopped her. 'Great sex is not love, Bianca,' he pointed out coldly. 'When are you going to learn that?'

She looked uncertain now. 'I... It's not just that,' she said. 'Surely not...'

Adam's frustration was acute. To place his heart in her hands was unthinkable, no matter how much he was tempted. She had no idea of true love. No damned idea! Dear God, if he let her, she'd tear his heart out completely. She'd already broken it a dozen times over.

'Don't try to make the last fortnight into more than it was, Bianca,' he continued harshly. 'Your mother's gone away happy and we had a great time together. Let's leave it at that.'

'You mean you...you don't want us to...to continue?'

'I didn't say that,' he said roughly. 'But let's not romanticise our relationship. We're friends and flatmates who've discovered we're sexually compatible.'

'Sexually compatible,' she repeated, rather blankly.

Exasperation at her lack of insight had him pulling her against him and kissing her with more impatience than passion. 'There,' he growled, once he'd reduced her to trembling. 'That's sex, Bianca, not love. What we've been doing every night in bed is sex, not love. What we did in the penthouse was sex, not love. Get the picture?'

'Oh, yes,' she said, and the hurt in her eyes nearly killed him. 'I get the picture. Your pretending to be my husband was just for sex. Your being nice to my mother was just for sex. Your buying me that car was just for sex. Yet all the while, down deep, stupid me thought it was because you loved me. You're sick, Adam Marsden. And cruel. Don't bother selling the unit and buying a house on my account. Because I won't be living in it with you. I won't be having sex with you any more either!'

Her tirade pained him terribly. He grimaced and went to say something, but she was too quick for him.

'Oh, don't bother trying to defend yourself,' she bit out. 'I recognise a right bastard when I see one. Occasionally it takes me a while, but once the penny drops, it stays dropped. Funny—all these years I admired and respected you so much. I might not have loved you as I love you now, but I always thought highly of you. Now I wouldn't spit on you if you were on fire!'

He couldn't bear her looking at him like that. He just couldn't bear it.

She wrenched out of his hands and started stalking off.

'Bianca, don't go!' he called after her.

But she kept on walking.

'I love you!' he confessed aloud with a tortured groan. 'I've always loved you. You must know that...'

She stopped, then slowly turned, scepticism warring with hope on her ravaged face. 'Don't say that if you don't mean it.'

His shoulders squared and he looked her straight in the eye. 'I mean it,' he said, looking strong on the outside while inside he was unravelling. Dear God, he'd done it now. He'd really done it.

Well, if he was going to burn his bridge behind him he was sure as hell going to get across that bridge first. He began walking towards her with a purposeful stride.

'I love you,' he repeated, his eyes locking hard with hers. 'And I don't want you to go.'

She fell into his arms, as he'd known she would. Bianca, he realised resignedly, *was* a romantic. What a pity her commitment never matched her ardour. It was a case of the flesh being willing, but the future being weak.

But, oh . . . that ardour . . . and that flesh.

He gathered her to him and began wallowing in both.

CHAPTER TWELVE

BIANCA had never felt so happy. Adam loved her. He'd *always* loved her, he'd said. All those qualms she'd been having over his treatment of her lately had already disappeared in the face of that love.

She lay back in the bubble bath and soaked in her happiness. Even her qualms about *this* place had been put to rest. He'd finally admitted that he owned the penthouse. He'd bought it a few years back while he was still living at home and market prices were down.

He hadn't paid cash for it, of course, just a deposit, then mortgaged the rest and rented it out for a tidy sum to a yuppy American insurance executive who'd been over here for a three-year stint in Sydney. When that lease had expired, two months ago, Adam had come in to do some repainting and redecorating and found himself staying over on the odd night, because he liked the place. But he planned on renting it out again soon.

It wasn't an orgy palace, he'd told her. Even if it looked a bit like one in some ways. Everything was so large and lush and plush—from the thick carpet to the huge bed to the satin sheets.

Bianca glanced around the equally large and opulent-looking bathroom, with its sunken spa bath

144

and huge shower which could house an orgy itself
if it wanted. She smiled idly as her toes played with
the gold taps, which were shaped like dolphins.

What did it matter if Adam *had* brought Sophie
here, she mused, or any of those bimbos he'd once
dated? He hadn't loved them. He loved her. He'd
always loved her, she reminded herself, revelling in
the way that made her feel. So very, very special.

Any negative feelings—if there were any—in this
wonderful new relationship with Adam were over
her own past treatment of *him*. The knowledge that
he had indeed always loved her filled her with some
guilt, plus a very real need to make it up to him.
She didn't deserve such loyalty and such an en-
during love, but, since Adam saw fit to lavish such
a love on her, she wasn't about to reject it. But she
wanted to spoil him shamelessly in return for having
put up with her all these years.

So thinking, she rose from the bath, towelling
herself dry then massaging some perfumed mois-
turiser into her skin before pulling on the red and
white kimono Adam had insisted she bring with her
tonight.

He liked it on her, he said. And he liked her hair
up the way she did it sometimes, piled haphazardly
on top of her head, with bits and pieces falling
around her face and neck.

She fixed it that way, and made herself up similarly to the way the girl had made her up that
Saturday Adam had taken her to the races—with
plenty of eye make-up, blusher and bold red lips.

She surveyed the finished product in the vanity mirror, conceding that she looked...colourful.

A downward glance at her reflection noted the peaked nipples pressing against the silk. Two weeks ago she might have thought it was this provocative place turning her on, or the champagne she'd already downed—Adam had bought a bottle on his way here and opened it on arrival.

But it wasn't her surroundings or the alcohol which was causing her blood to fizz and her skin to tingle. It was love. She loved Adam as she had never loved a man before. With her heart as well as her body. He was everything a girl could want. The complete man. Basically good and kind and decent, but also beautiful to look at, with a wickedly sexy side which was as fascinating as it was fun.

She blushed as she thought of how assertive he could be when aroused. How...masterful. But Adam being masterful was not what she planned for this evening. It was *her* turn to be masterful, she decided. And his to be pampered. And loved. And made love to.

'Adam, where are you?' she called out as she came out of the bathroom, feeling a little nervy. She'd never played this role before, but was determined to do it boldly, and with flair.

'In here,' Adam called back from the direction of the living room.

It was in darkness, the only light the lights of the city shining through the window. Bianca sucked in a steadying breath and padded her way across the white shag-pile carpet.

The lounge setting was white too, a deep, low four-cushioned sofa flanked by two two-seaters, all with a view of the bridge, the harbour and the city beyond. The bridge was the focus at that moment, with its coathanger shape outlined against the clear night sky and a steady stream of cars moving like strangely regimented glow-worms from one side of the city to the other.

'You like watching the lights?' she asked as she approached his seated form.

His legs were stretched out in front of her, his arms along the back of the sofa. He was wearing jeans and a white T-shirt which hugged and displayed his muscles without help or artifice. Bianca still could not understand how she hadn't noticed his lovely body till recently. It was certainly a case of none so blind as they who will not see.

He glanced over at her, then stared, his steel-grey eyes glittering in the dim light. She hoped it was with desire. But she could not afford to question whether it was or not. She had to assume.

Swallowing, she walked around in front of him and sidled between his thighs, kneeling down and leaning forward to spread her hands over his T-shirted chest, revelling in the feel of the hard, broad planes underneath the thin material.

'What are you doing?' he asked. A tad agitatedly, she thought, for her palms had just grazed his male nipples.

'Shh,' she murmured, her tongue suddenly thick in her throat. 'I'm having fun.'

'Oh, I see.' She wasn't sure if she liked the way his mouth lifted at one corner. His expression was vaguely cynical. 'And am I going to have fun too?'

She reached up to smooth her fingertips over his lips, wiping the smirk away. 'You will if you're a good boy and just do as you're told.' She ran a sharply nailed fingertip down his throat and down his chest towards the waistband of his jeans.

He sucked in breath sharply. 'What if I don't want to be a good boy?'

She smiled a wicked smile. 'Then I'll have to punish you. You know what happens to bad boys, don't you?'

He was staring at her as though mesmerised. 'No,' he said thickly. 'What?'

She took his hand and, rising slowly to her feet, pulled him up with her. 'They're made to have a bath.'

'A *what*?'

'A bath. I'm going to give you a bath.'

His chuckle held a secret darkness which teased her curiosity and inflamed her jealousy. 'Is there something wrong with my giving you a bath?' she asked archly. 'Has some other woman done that for you here?'

'No, no. You're the first, believe me. *Anywhere*. At least the first since I turned ten. I wouldn't even let my mother in the bathroom with me after that, and certainly not my sisters.'

'Oh? What happened when you turned ten?'

'I started growing in certain areas,' he said drily.

'And you grew very nicely in those certain areas too,' she complimented him as she led him towards the still steamy spa bath.

He actually blushed but she pretended not to see.

'You're not going to undress me, are you?' he asked, sounding a little panicky.

'But of course! What would be the fun in your undressing yourself?'

'What, indeed?' he said in a droll tone.

She threw him a questioning look as she stripped the T-shirt over his head. What was wrong with him? Wasn't he liking what she was doing? He *seemed* to be, by the look of the bulge in his jeans. Maybe he just felt a little unnerved at not being the one in control. She could imagine that most men were like that.

She slid her hands over his bare chest and looked up at him. 'Don't you want me to do this, Adam?' she asked gently. 'I mean... I thought you'd like it. I was going to wash you, and dry you, then give you a massage, and then...' She gulped down the sudden lump in her throat. She hoped she'd have the courage to go through with all she had in mind—if he let her. 'I... I only wanted to please you...'

When his eyes closed tightly for a second, panic gripped in her heart, but then they opened and they were amused and smiling. He took her hand and placed it on the snap fastening of his jeans. 'Be gentle with me,' he murmured.

Relief had her laughing a low, throaty, sexy laugh. 'Don't worry. I wouldn't want to damage the equipment.'

Adam lay back in the bath, his last fantasy about Bianca coming true. She had stayed out of the bath for quite a while, kneeling beside him and washing his back and body in true geisha style. But gradually her kimono had become water-spattered, and he'd spied those magnificent nipples of hers poking through the wet silk.

The temptation to lean over and take one into his mouth through the material had proved too much for him. It hadn't taken long after that for him to peel the whole damned kimono off her trembling body and insist she climb into the bath with him.

Now she was sitting behind him, her legs wrapped with seductive sensuousness around his hips. It was erotic in the extreme to feel her open like that and pressed up against his buttocks. His fierce awareness of that area, plus her trailing a wet soapy sponge over his front, from his own hardened nipples to his even harder privates was both agony and ecstasy.

'A massage, you said?' he suggested at last, though God knew how he was going to stand that. Talk about self-torture!

He stood it quite well. For it was bearable bliss—provided he lay on his stomach. He kept his eyes shut, though. The image of her doing what she was doing in the nude was bad enough, but the knowledge that if he turned his head to the left side, with his eyes open, he would be able to see her in the mirrored wall, was perturbing in the extreme.

'Higher,' he ordered thickly, then groaned when what felt like her nipples brushed over his buttocks. It was too much for him, and his eyes half opened. He peered through the glazed half-slits at the sight of her, straddled across his thighs, her hard-tipped breasts swinging gently back and forth as she kneaded his shoulders.

'That's enough,' he grated out. She stopped, and he rolled over beneath her spread thighs. Love and desire crashed through him at the sight of her flushed face and wildly glittering eyes. She was beautiful, his Bianca. But never so beautiful as at this moment, caught in the throes of a passion which she sincerely believed was for him. He would be a fool not to see that she really thought she loved him.

It evoked some hope in him that maybe this time...just maybe...her love might last. But then he recalled what she'd said to him out in the living room. 'Fun', she'd called it. Fun.

His heart hardened a little and he reached out to hand her the small foil packet he'd kept clenched in his fists.

'You do the honours,' he said, and gritted his teeth while she did. Expertly. Smoothly.

His own hypocrisy did not escape him, but still her skill annoyed him. Grasping her quite savagely by the hips, he lifted her up and angled her roughly down onto him.

Her gasp might have been a protest, or pleasure. He didn't know and told himself he didn't care. Blinding himself to anything but a determination to prove a point, he urged her to ride him, groaning with triumph when her initial hesitation was soon lost to her own soaring desire. He'd never asked this of her before, preferring to be the man on top up till now. But this time, he wanted to see for himself how wild a creature she was. And how wanton.

He watched her through narrowed eyes, trying to steel his heart against her, telling himself that this utter abandon had been witnessed and enjoyed by others before him, men she'd *thought* she loved. Where were they now, those men?

On the scrap heap of her life, that was where.

She stopped suddenly and smiled down at him, making him moan when she bent down to give him a long, lingering kiss.

'In case you've forgotten,' she murmured against his lips. 'I love you.'

And then she went back to what she'd been doing, her hips lifting and falling with athletic and sensuous rhythm, her eyes never leaving his. He saw them grow heavy, saw them glaze over as her climax grew near. Her lips parted to cry out his name as she came, and with that raw, naked cry his body and his heart gave an answering burst of love for her once more.

He pulled her down on top of him afterwards, and buried his face in her hair lest she see his despair. For he would never love anyone as he loved her. He didn't know what he would do if she ever left him. The thought was unthinkable.

'Adam,' she whispered, making no attempt to remove him from her body.

'What?'

'I want you to know that I've never done that before. Been on top, I mean.'

He grasped her face and lifted it so that he could see her eyes. 'That's the honest to goodness truth?' he said, amazed yet moved. For he could see she wasn't lying. He'd always known when Bianca was lying. She could never really look him in the eye when she was telling fibs.

'I know you think I'm some kind of sex-crazed fool who used to fall at the feet of every muscle-bound bum who came my way, but that's not true, Adam. I haven't had that many boyfriends either. There've been times when many, many months have gone by and I've been all by myself.

'I never picked up any men during my back-packing treks overseas. I'm not that stupid! And even when I *was* involved with someone back home here, I never felt comfortable enough to do what I did today. I was always a bit self-conscious about taking the assertive role in sex. Frankly, I was too shy to be on top.'

Disbelief at what she was saying warred with his very deep need to believe her. '*You*, Bianca? *Shy?*'

'In some things I am. I . . . I've never been happy with my boobs. Or my lack of them. Fact is, I've never thought my body was much cop at all.'

'But you have a gorgeous little body!' he exclaimed. 'I think it's quite perfect.'

'I know you do,' she said, her heart turning over. 'That's why I dared to expose myself to you today in the most intimate way a woman can expose herself to a man. I wanted you to see me making love to you, to see how much I loved you.'

'Oh, Bianca . . .'

'You do believe me, Adam, don't you?' she asked, a little worried by the clouds of doubt which kept flitting across his face.

He said nothing for a moment, and when he smiled there was something incredibly sad about it. 'Of course I believe you. And I'm incredibly touched.'

'Tell me you love me, Adam,' she insisted, something about this conversation prompting panic in her heart. 'Tell me you'll always love me.'

Why did he sigh? Why did he sound almost . . . resigned? And that smile again . . . that sad, sad smile.

'I love you, Bianca,' he said, and no one could have doubted the wealth of emotion in his raw voice. 'I'll *always* love you.'

Bianca sighed a deep, shuddering sigh of relief. 'Then let's go home, my darling,' she murmured. 'This is all very nice here, but it's not real life, is it?'

CHAPTER THIRTEEN

REAL life with Bianca, Adam soon decided, was great—despite an initial qualm that she might become bored with him once their relationship settled into a more regular routine.

Both of them returned to work on the Monday, after spending Sunday looking at houses and moving that lucky little dog, Lucky, out of the veterinary hospital and into some boarding kennels along Mona Vale Road, only fifteen minutes' drive away from his besotted new owner.

Monday evening was very pleasantly spent at home watching a movie on television after dinner before they finally went to bed, where Adam made love to Bianca with a leisurely passion compatible with his surprisingly relaxed and happy state.

Bianca seemed to like it, for she curled up against him and went to sleep straight away afterwards. For his part Adam found it a bit of a relief not to have to play the role of bad-boy lover extraordinaire. It was rather nice to have simple straightforward sex, full of tenderness and love. Who knew? Maybe Bianca was ready for this kind of relationship. Maybe she'd finally grown up where love was concerned.

Tuesday evening passed pretty well the same way, although there wasn't much on television, so they listened to music and chattered about the books they'd been reading. They'd always been very comfortable in each other's company and that had never changed.

They liked the same kind of movies on the whole, and the same kind of books, although Bianca was more into Stephen King than he was. They both liked fantasy fiction, with some adventure and romance thrown in. Only in music did they differ largely—Adam preferring jazz and country and western to Bianca's passion for pop and rock.

He came home early from work on the Wednesday—it was the last week of the term and things were really winding down—only to find Bianca already home from her office. She was sprawled out in the lounge, looking rather down in the mouth.

'What's up?' he asked, and dropped a kiss on that mouth as he sat down on the edge of the wide-cushioned sofa.

'I feel yukky,' she said.

'Yukky in what way?'

'Yukky in the stomach. I kept thinking I was going to heave up all day, but I didn't. Still, in the end the boss sent me home, since I was spending so much time in the toilet waiting for it to happen.'

'Hmm. I feel all right, so it can't be last night's dinner. Maybe you've got a virus. Poor Bianca,' he murmured, stroking her hair back from her forehead. 'You do look peaky. Perhaps you should go to a doctor, have yourself checked out.'

She gave him the oddest look. 'Maybe...'

'Don't worry about cooking anything tonight,' he said. 'I'll pick up some takeaway. I dare say you don't feel like eating much.'

'God, no. Nothing at all.'

She fell silent, frowning, and Adam had the feeling she was away in another world. It wasn't like Bianca to be sick. Or to be silent. Something was bothering her, but it seemed he wasn't to be privy to what it was.

He stayed sitting and stroking her hair and she closed her eyes, turning her face a little away from him. He was not a body language expert, but that small gesture bothered him. It felt like a physical as well as an emotional rejection.

The thought that Bianca wouldn't want him to make love to her that night was more perturbing than it should have been. He was being paranoid, he knew, but the niggling suspicion that there was more here than met the eye would not go away.

'Before I forget,' he said at last, taking his hand away. 'There's an end-of-year party of the faculty at the university on Friday night, so I'll be home late.'

Bianca opened her eyes and turned her head back with a sigh. 'That's all right,' she said, still not really looking at him. 'I'll have a drink with the people from work. They all go down to the pub after work on a Friday. Or I'll go to the gym if I'm feeling better by then. No doubt this is only a twenty-four-hour tummy bug.'

And it was. She felt much better the next day, she said, though she was still a little preoccupied, walking out of the door without kissing him goodbye as she had on the previous three mornings.

Adam vowed to ask her what was bothering her that evening, but no sooner was dinner over than an old girlfriend rang out of the blue—God knew where she'd got the number!—and Bianca talked and talked to her for simply hours.

Her name was Roberta, and she was one of the girls Bianca had gone backpacking around the world with—the sort of outrageously flip female one would never imagine settling down. But apparently she'd fallen in love with her dentist—poor bloke—and was getting married. From Bianca's side of the conversation, Adam gathered the stupid girl was pregnant as well, which was good for another hour's chit-chat about babies and such.

Adam went to bed on his own in the end, feeling quite resentful that Bianca preferred talking to a girlfriend than being with him. He was also beginning to feel vaguely unsettled by the atmosphere in general.

Was the rot already setting in?

He was coming to think so, lying there still wide awake when Bianca finally came to bed, though he pretended to be asleep. So he was pleasantly surprised when she snuggled in behind him, her hands wrapping lovingly around his body, her fingers ca-ressing his chest and stomach.

When he groaned and rolled over and reached for her, he was taken aback when she said no, she didn't want to make love, she just wanted to touch him and hold him. Was that all right by him?

He said of course it was, but, while he enjoyed the feel of her hands touching and holding him, there was something strangely platonic in the whole scenario. It was as though she was telling him something with her hands—something he didn't want to hear. I love you, they seemed to be saying. But not the same way as I was loving you a week ago. That old spark has gone out. The sexual chemistry has died.

Adam lay there long after Bianca drifted off to sleep, lay there with his body aching and his heart breaking.

He could not bring himself to talk to her in the morning as they went about their breakfasts. She didn't seem to notice, her mind off in the clouds again. Or was it something far more down-to-earth which was occupying her mind? he began to think with savage jealousy. Had she met someone else? Was she trying to find some way to tell stupid old Adam to get lost?

'You're very quiet,' he said at last through gritted teeth.

Bianca looked up from her plate of muesli, something like guilt in her eyes. 'Am I? Sorry. I was thinking...'

'About what?'

'Oh . . . this and that.'

'Care to enlighten me on what "this and that" means?' he quizzed, trying not to sound suspicious and accusing.

She opened her mouth, then shut it again. 'It's nothing to worry *you* about,' she muttered. 'Yet.'

'That sounds very mysterious. When can I hope to know this dark little secret of yours?'

She actually blushed, and Adam's stomach tightened. Bianca blushing was as alien a concept as her staying in love.

'What makes you think I have a dark little secret?' she said.

'I know you very well, Bianca,' he returned ruefully. 'I can read you like a book sometimes.'

'No one knows anybody else all that well, Adam,' she mused cryptically. 'If we did we wouldn't flounder around, not knowing what to do and what to say sometimes.'

Now what did she mean by *that*? Was she afraid of his reaction if she broke up with him? Was she worried he wouldn't go as easily as dear old Derek?

Well, she was right there. He bloody well wouldn't! If the worst came to the worst he would revert to Adam Marsden, bastard of the month. No way was he letting Bianca slip out of his hands now. Hell, he'd get her pregnant if he had to. Though God knows how he'd manage that, with her taking the pill.

Thinking of the pill reminded him that Bianca
hadn't had a period for a while, and a thought suddenly clicked. She could be suffering from PMT.
She'd complained and complained about the effect
the pill had on her, especially in the week leading
up to her period. Her breasts would be sore, she'd
have a bloated stomach and a yukky feeling.

Yes, of course—that was it! Why hadn't he
thought of it before? Bianca had always been
touchy about her body and her periods.

His relief was huge as he reached over to place
a soothing hand on top of hers. 'If you're worried
about the intimate side of our relationship once you
get your period, then don't be. I know I was demanding at the beginning of this new relationship
of ours, but I do realise things can't always be like
that.'

She blinked at him. 'What? Oh, yes. Good.
Thank you. That . . . that's a relief off my mind.'
She stood up and moved swiftly over to the kitchen
counter. 'Can I get you another cup of coffee?'

'No, I'd better get going. Don't forget I'll be late
tonight,' he reminded her. 'It's sure to be at least
ten before I can get away, which means it will be
closer to eleven by the time I get home.'

'No sweat.' She didn't look up, her concentration on pouring boiling water into her mug.

He came over and gave her a peck on the cheek.
'Wait up for me, will you?'

She slanted him a quick smile, but he could feel
the tension in her. 'Yes, of course.'

Adam could have bitten his tongue for seemingly putting sexual pressure on her when it was obvious she was not feeling the best. Yet, despite his guilt, an oddly desperate feeling suddenly swept over him, and as soon as she put the kettle down he pulled her into his arms, kissing her hungrily for a few seconds.

'How's that for a goodbye kiss?' he said stupidly and, whirling, strode out of the unit before he made even more of a fool of himself.

Bianca stayed on his mind all morning—and all afternoon. By the time the faculty party started that evening, he was a dead loss where being social and charming were concerned. He was worried about the woman he loved. There was something wrong. He just felt it.

'Sorry,' he told his chums over his first drink. 'But I simply can't stay. Family emergency.'

He dropped into the pub at Crows Nest on the way home, but Bianca hadn't joined her colleagues there that night, he was told. She wasn't at home either, so it seemed likely she was down at the gym.

The gym was Bianca's therapist. Whenever she was troubled or upset, she would work out. She'd once told him exercise was good for PMT, so it was likely she was down there, pumping iron or doing her third step class. That girl sometimes didn't know when to stop.

He decided to go down and stop her.

The gym was within walking distance of their block of units—Bianca always jogged down and back—but Adam was in a hurry so he drove down. He slid his BMW into the kerb opposite, switched off the engine and was about to climb out when Bianca came through the swinging front doors, dressed in purple lycra bike shorts and a matching midriff top.

Adam might have called out to her if she'd been alone.

But she wasn't.

Dear old Derek was with her, dressed in shiny blue boxer shorts and a black singlet top designed to show off his huge chest. He also had one of his huge arms solidly around her shoulder, and she was leaning into him as though for all the world she wanted them to become one right there on the pavement.

Adam wanted to kill them both, so he counted to ten—after which he still wanted to kill them both.

Don't jump to conclusions, he kept telling himself as he watched Derek fold Bianca into the low passenger seat of a sports car which matched its owner's shorts for colour and shininess, watched with a pounding heart and seething soul as they drove off together.

Adam might have scorched after them in the BMW if he'd been pointing the right way. As it was, the shiny blue Mazda accelerated away before he could say 'kill' and was gone. He sat there for simply ages, trying to get his black fury under control. Or was it black despair?

No, not despair. Despair didn't feel like this. Despair wanted to run and hide and cry, whereas Adam wanted to seize and strangle and scream!

She would have to come home eventually, he decided at last, with a cold calm that was as frightening as it was chillingly satisfying.

And when she did...

He drove home with seeming composure, only to have it shattered by the sight of Derek's car parked outside their block of units. She'd brought him *here*? A glance upwards at the unit showed that the lights were on in the front living room and master bedroom. As he watched the light in the bedroom clicked out.

Adam's pain knew no bounds. He could not believe she could be this wicked. Or this cruel! It was bad enough she'd taken up with Derek again, but to do so in *his* flat, and in *their* bed!

The only reason he didn't go upstairs then and there was because he knew he would not be responsible for what he did. She wasn't worth going to jail for life over.

What to do? How to handle it?

He stayed in his car and waited till Derek left at around ten-thirty. Then he waited till well after midnight, making sure Bianca would be asleep when he went in.

Icy tentacles wound round his heart as he stared down at her, curled up with seeming innocence in the middle of the bed. How could she just go off to sleep after what she'd done? Still, sex did exhaust one, he thought bitterly.

He hated having to climb into that bed with her, knowing what he knew, but it had to be done. Vengeance had to wait till morning. Besides, he wasn't ever going to let her suspect he'd witnessed her treachery. His male ego could not take that kind of punishment.

Lying there beside her, unable to sleep, he wondered how long she'd been planning to juggle both of them.

It wasn't like Bianca to be this treacherous, Adam agonised. To give her credit, she usually only had one lover at a time. And she was usually tremendously loyal while she was with her one and only. This type of deceit and double-dealing was something entirely new to her character.

Her mood over the past couple of days suddenly explained itself. She was feeling guilty. Very, very guilty.

But guilt hadn't stopped her from having her fun tonight, had it? Obviously she hadn't been as happy with the tender loving sex he'd been giving her this week as he'd thought she'd been.

'Adam?' she said dreamily from her half-sleep. 'Is that you?'

'Who else?' he bit out.

She yawned and rolled over. 'Did you have a nice party?'

Not as nice as yours, he thought savagely.

Shock crashed through him when she began to stroke his thigh. He stiffened in more ways than one.

'Too tired?' she asked when his hand abruptly closed over hers, only inches from the evidence of his unwanted and involuntary arousal.

'Let's just say I'm not in the mood.'

'Oh...'

Adam's resentment over her reaction to his rejection was acute. How dared she sound hurt? And how dare *he* still be tempted?

'Too much whisky,' he muttered, and rolled his back to her.

'You shouldn't drink and drive, you know, Adam,' she said, now actually sounding worried about him. Was there no limit to her perfidy?

'Yeah, well, there are a lot of things people shouldn't do, Bianca,' he growled, giving some vent to his simmering outrage. 'But that doesn't stop them. It's not a nice world. Now let me go to sleep, for pity's sake. I don't know about you but I'm wrecked.'

More than wrecked. Totally destroyed. But she would never know that. Come morning, she would be out on her ear, never knowing what she'd done wrong!

CHAPTER FOURTEEN

BIANCA woke the next morning with butterflies in her stomach and trepidation in her heart. Who would have believed her being pregnant by Adam would cause her so much concern? It wasn't that she wasn't happy about it. She was. She was ecstatic. It was Adam's possible reaction which worried her.

A few days ago she would have been positive Adam would be just as thrilled. Now ... she wasn't so sure.

What was it Roberta had said the other night? How once you really fell in love you couldn't wait to get married, settle down and have a baby with the person you loved? While such sentiments coincided exactly with what *she'd* been feeling lately, Bianca wasn't at all sure Adam felt the same way. He hadn't once mentioned marriage, despite his agreeing to buy a house so she could bring Lucky to live with them.

Then last night ...

Bianca threw a worried glance over at Adam's still sleeping form and bit her bottom lip. Adam had been *very* late home. He'd said he'd been drinking whisky but he hadn't smelt of alcohol at all. He'd been lying to her. And then he hadn't wanted to make love.

Had he been with someone else? Had Sophie loomed on the horizon again, with her big boobs and highly accommodating nature?

Bianca heaved in a deep breath then let it out again with a shuddering sigh. Immediately Adam rolled over, settling oddly cold grey eyes upon her.

'Oh,' Bianca said. 'I...I thought you were still asleep. I was just about to get up and make coffee, but I have to go to the toilet first.' She scrambled out of bed, dragging on her kimono before dashing for the bathroom.

When she returned, Adam was still looking at her in that peculiarly cold fashion. 'Is there something wrong?' she asked as she sashed the kimono tightly around her waist.

'That depends.' He stretched, then linked his arms up under his head.

'On what?'

'On how you're going to handle what I have to say.'

A nameless fear gripped Bianca's insides. She tried to keep her cool but it was hard. 'Then perhaps you'd better just say it. Whatever it is you have to say...'

'Very well. This isn't going to work out, Bianca.'

Bianca swallowed. 'What isn't going to work out?'

'You. Me. Us.'

Spots began to swim around Bianca's eyes. 'Why not?' she choked out.

He sat up abruptly, throwing back the quilt and swinging his feet over the side of the bed. His face, she noted, was uncompromisingly hard. He shrugged on his red dressing gown then stood up, looming over her.

'Too much water's gone under the bridge with us, I'm afraid,' he said. 'I loved you for a long time, Bianca. I thought I still did. But I see now I don't. It was a hangover from the past.

'I wanted you for such a long time and ... well, now I've had you—and while it was very satisfying in one way it wasn't quite as good as I'd anticipated. To be brutally honest, Bianca, my fires for you have burnt out at long last. There's no spark left in me. No ... chemistry. I'm sorry. There's no use my pretending. I think, under the circumstances, you should find somewhere else to live.'

Bianca blinked her utter bewilderment while the blood began to drain from her face. Nausea swirled in her stomach. 'But ... but you said you loved me. You said you would *always* love me.'

His shrug was flippant in the extreme. 'Looks like I made a mistake. Sorry.'

Bianca thought of the kiss he'd given her yesterday morning, that awful parody of passion which had been a real goodbye kiss in a way she'd never dreamt he meant at the time.

'No ... no, I'm the one who's sorry,' she said weakly, despair hot on the heels of dismay. She had never known such heartache. 'I'm sorry I ever met you...'

'Come on, Bianca, don't dramatise. It's just your pride that's hurt. You'll bounce back, right onto the next fellow. It's not as though you crave permanence, my love. Or commitment. Life is just a ball to you, remember? It's for having fun. Well, we had fun, didn't we? Don't be such a little hypocrite.'

Something rang in her whirling head—some bell which warned her that this wasn't her Adam talking.

All those moments they'd shared this past week— those warm, incredibly tender moments—flooded back into her brain, telling her that *that* was the real Adam, not this heartless stranger who was telling her oh, so casually that everything she'd ever meant to him was dead and that it shouldn't bother her one bit.

But when she looked into his face, searching for a hint of guilt or conscience, she saw nothing but a mask of stony indifference.

Bile rose in her throat and her hand fluttered up to try to stop it from going further. But in vain. 'I...I'm going to be sick,' she choked out, and, whirling, dashed for the bathroom.

She made it to the toilet bowl just in time, though there was nothing substantial to heave into it.

Afterwards she slumped against the cold tiled floor, her head resting limply against the toilet-roll holder on the wall. She felt drained, yet not nearly as despairing as she'd been a minute ago. For during her flight to the bathroom Bianca had caught a glimpse of them both reflected in the vanity mirror.

She had looked distressed, but *Adam* had looked *devastated*, his shoulders sagging, his face twisted with self-disgust.

But it was his eyes ... oh, his eyes ...

They'd clung to her back as she'd fled, clung with such pained regret and yearning, as though he wished he could cut out his tongue.

Which meant what? Bianca puzzled anew. He was being cruel to be kind? Or could it be that he didn't believe she really loved him and was getting out before he got in too deep?

That was more like her Adam, she conceded sadly, and her heart turned over with love and understanding for the man. She'd put him through so much over the years. Too much, perhaps. She could well appreciate his lack of faith in her.

But that didn't mean she was about to let him go—certainly not into the arms of a female vulture like that Sophie creature. He was the father of her baby, and he was going to marry her if it was the last thing he did!

'Are you all right?' Adam called casually from the bedroom.

Bianca gathered all her courage, got to her feet, rinsed out her mouth with mouthwash, pursed her lips in defiance of her pounding heart and flounced back into the bedroom, her hands finding her hips as she glared over at where Adam was sitting on the side of the bed, pretending to look totally unconcerned.

At least...she *hoped* he was pretending.

'No, I'm not all right, you unfeeling bastard. I happen to be pregnant, with *your* baby. I also happen to still love you, regardless of that appalling speech you just delivered.

'Before you ask, I haven't been on the pill since last month. That first time we made love and you didn't use protection seems to have done the impossible. Made *me* into a mother. And I have no intention of having an abortion so don't even ask.

'As I said, I love you and I want to keep our baby, and if you're halfway the decent man I think you are, you'll do the right thing and marry me.'

She scooped in a much needed breath before continuing. 'Which reminds me—I don't believe all that garbage about your not loving me. You *do* love me, Adam Marsden. I have no doubts about that at all!'

Bianca was taken aback by the black fury which swept across his face. 'And I have no doubt about that either,' he snarled, re-sashing his dressing gown as he stood up.

Bianca suspected the savage action was to keep his hands busy, otherwise they might have reached out and strangled her, so murderous was the look on his face.

'Because of course you're quite right!' he grated out. 'I do still love you—curse my stupid masochistic self to hell! I also thought I knew you pretty well, but not in my wildest dreams would I have imagined you could be this wicked. Or this coldly calculating.'

Bianca was staggered by his counter-accusations. Wicked? Coldly calculating? Anyone would think she'd deliberately gone out and got pregnant!

'Enough that you used me to back up the lies you told your mother,' he raged on. 'Enough that you told me you loved me when we both know you didn't.'

'That's not tr—'

'Shut up!' he roared. 'I won't listen to your lies any more. I can see it all now. You deliberately didn't mention protection that night till afterwards, knowing full well I'd be so carried away by finally making love to you, the only girl I'd ever loved in my whole life, that it would be the last thing on my mind. And you did it because you suspected you were already pregnant by Derek. You were hedging your bets, Bianca. You wanted an each way chance at winning a husband for yourself and a father for your baby.'

'*What?*'

'Oh, don't play the innocent with me. The wool's finally lifted from my eyes. You think I didn't notice the change in you these past few days? You decided you wanted Derek back, didn't you? You'd grown bored with me. But he wouldn't have you back, would he? Or marry you!

'You told him about your pregnancy last night and he gave you the shove. So it fell back onto good old Adam to see to the aid of the party. You even thought you'd soften me up with some more sex before dropping the bombshell. One thing I'd like to know, though. Did you try that tactic with Derek last night too? I'll bet he didn't knock you back, did he? There again, he isn't mug enough to love you.'

Her hand cracked across his face with all her considerable strength. It rocked him, but Bianca couldn't see anything much through her haze of hurt and anger.

'This is *your* baby, you fool, not Derek's!' she told him, her voice shaking uncontrollably. 'I never had unprotected sex with Derek, nor any kind of sex at *all* with Derek for that matter. I was going to that weekend up at Foster, but I changed my mind. I told you before, Adam. I am not promiscuous!

'As for last night, the truth is I fainted down at the gym. Derek was there and insisted on taking me home. He really was very sweet and understanding. He even drove to an all-night chemist and bought me a pregnancy testing kit, then came back and waited while I confirmed what I had already suspected.

'I asked him to stay for a cup of coffee and he told me how happy he was that you and I had decided to stop our silly "open marriage" and have a baby. In case you've forgotten, my mother told him we were married.'

Tears pricked her eyes at the thought. For they would never be married now. 'I wasn't trying to soften you up with sex when you came home,' she said in a strangled voice. 'I wanted to make love with the father of my baby, the only man I've ever really loved.

'If I've been different the last couple of days, it was because I was worried that you hadn't mentioned marriage. I was afraid you might not want our baby. I was afraid you might not want me as your wife. I was...just...afraid...'

She started to cry then, great racking sobs which shook her body from head to toe.

Adam's arms around her sent her collapsing against him. 'Oh, Adam...Adam,' she cried. 'How could you believe all those terrible things about me?'

Yes, how could he?

Adam had never felt this rotten or this wonderful all at the same time. No one could have doubted her sincerity just now. The truth had shone from her impassioned face for all to see—but most for him to see.

She loved him. She wanted to marry him. She was going to have his baby.

His baby...

His arms tightened around her. He tried to speak but couldn't for a while, so he let his hands and lips speak for him as he stroked her back and kissed the top of her head.

'So when are you going to make an honest man out of me?' he murmured at last.

Her head rose slowly, heart-rending doubt on her tear-ravaged face. 'You ... you don't *have* to marry me, Adam. If you think that I don't really love you then perhaps we should wait a while to tie the knot ...'

'No no,' he denied swiftly as panic rose in his heart. 'I don't want to wait. I want you as my wife as soon as possible.' That rebellious pout to her lips had begun to worry the life out of him.

'No, I don't think that's such a good idea. I think we definitely should wait a while ... till you're sure ...'

Adam groaned, then sighed his resignation to her stubbornness. He could only blame himself, he supposed. And his lack of faith in her. Besides, he'd waited this long. He could wait a little longer.

'But meanwhile we *will* be moving into a house together, won't we?' he said, trying to sound masterful.

'But of course! We have a dog and a baby to consider.'

Adam smiled wryly as he thought of that damned dog. Still, he guessed a family wasn't a proper family without a dog. He'd have to sell the penthouse if they were going to buy that really great house near the beach they'd looked at the previous weekend. Which was a shame. He'd really enjoyed his times there with Bianca.

But that didn't mean he couldn't find other places to take her. He had a feeling he'd better not ever get complacent where Bianca and sex were concerned. She'd liked the bad boy side of him far more than she would probably ever admit. He'd rather liked it himself.

He made a mental note to find out all the plush and decadent-looking hotels around Sydney where a man could take his lady-love for a night of sin. Maybe he would suss one out for tonight.

'What are you smiling at?' she asked suspiciously.

'Nothing. I was just thinking I'd like to take you out somewhere to celebrate tonight. A hotel, perhaps. We could have a romantic candlelit dinner, break open a bottle or two of champagne, then retire to the honeymoon suite.'

'But we're not honeymooners!'

'Who cares? They'll think we are. All the men will stare at you and envy me like mad. Which reminds me...there's a certain red dress I bought which I'd like you to wear...'

EPILOGUE

A WARM November sun was shining when Bianca finally emerged from the house and walked sedately down their backyard along the strip of red carpet laid especially for the occasion.

Adam stared at her and thought he'd never seen her look more breathtakingly beautiful or ravishingly radiant. Her white bridal gown was classically elegant, made of silk, straight and slender, with an off-the-shoulder neckline and a cleavage on display which made his heart beat a little quicker.

Having a baby had matured Bianca's figure somewhat.

She wasn't wearing a veil—Adam was privately surprised he'd talked her into a long white dress—though her long black hair was braided down her back with delicate white flowers set into each twist. The pearl choker and earrings he'd bought her as a wedding gift looked superb against her tanned skin.

And well they should, he thought wryly. They had cost all of his winnings so far this year. Over thirty thousand dollars.

Bianca had no idea how much they had cost. Or how much he still gambled. She'd worry if she knew. But Adam knew what he was doing, and it gave him great pleasure to be able to afford to lavish such an expensive gift on her on this marvellous day.

Still, perhaps it was time to give some of the gambling up, especially the races. It was becoming more and more difficult to return a profit there, and, frankly, it was far too time-consuming.

He might even give up the casino as well. After all, he no longer had any need of extra money, having recently accepted a new job at Brisbane University which involved a considerable rise in prestige and salary. A house went with the job as well, which meant they could rent out this house while they lived up there.

Bianca was very excited about the move. She loved new places and new 'adventures'.

Bianca...

God, how he loved her—now more than ever. Perhaps because he was now absolutely certain that she loved him back, with a love that would last. She'd been right to make him wait. Marrying her today was going to be the best day of his life— other than the day his son had been born, of course.

He sent a quick glance over to where fifteen-month-old Tony was sitting next to his grand-mother in the first line of chairs, his small chubby arms wrapped tightly around Lucky's scruffy, fluffy neck.

Adam's face filled with loving exasperation. They were inseparable, those two. He'd nearly had a fit when Lucky had first leapt up over the railing into

Tony's cot a couple of months back, and settled down for an afternoon nap with his young master. But every time he'd tried to eject the dog, his son had screamed.

Dog and boy won the day, though never had a dog been so scrupulously wormed—or more often—not to mention bathed. Bianca called him an old worry-wart, and perhaps he was. Someone in the family had to do the worrying. Bianca certainly didn't. She was an eternal optimist.

He smiled over at his son, who smiled back, a wickedly naughty little grin which heralded that he was more his mother's offspring than his father's. Lord knew what would happen once Tony reached the terrible twos. He shuddered to think.

'You're supposed to be looking at the bride,' Bianca hissed as she reached his side.

'I was checking on your son,' he whispered back. 'Seeing if he was behaving himself.'

'Why is he always *my* son when you feel he needs checking on?'

Bianca smiled up into Adam's sheepish face and thought he had never looked so handsome, or so adorable. She reached up on tiptoe and kissed him.

'Hey,' he objected softly. 'That's supposed to come afterwards.'

She laughed. 'So's having children.'

'Children?' He eyed her warily. 'Are you trying to tell me something?'

'Could be. I haven't sighted a period for four months, and last night the line of my favourite test went blue again. On top of that my boobs are killing me, and while I was getting ready this morning I fainted. You know I never faint.'

'Except when you're pregnant.'

'That's right.'

Bianca was moved by the sight of Adam's joy as he grasped her hands and squeezed them.

'We'd better get married, then, don't you think?' he said thickly.

The celebrant noisily cleared her throat, indicating that she really did wish to marry this strange couple some time this century. Why they wanted everyone to think they were merely renewing their marriage vows, she had no idea! She knew for a fact that this was their first marriage ceremony. Still, hers was not to reason why—especially when she'd been paid so well for the small deception.

They finally stopped whispering and laughing, and the bride nodded for her to begin. She sighed and did so.

'We are gathered here on this lovely November afternoon, in this beautiful garden, to witness Adam and Bianca's renewal of their marriage vows. Bianca and Adam have written special words for the occasion. Adam?'

Bianca's heart contracted fiercely as Adam turned to take her hands, his face very serious all of a sudden.

'Bianca, my darling,' he said, his voice quavering a little. 'This is a very special day for me. A day which marks the beginning of the rest of my life with you as my wife. I promise always to love you. I will never be unfaithful to you. I promise to treasure you all the days of my life, my darling. Bianca, my love, I am yours.' And he bent to kiss her.

'And you, Bianca,' the celebrant prompted, suddenly having difficulty in stopping herself from crying. How had she ever thought this couple strange? They had to be the most romantic, most in-love pair she had ever seen in her life!

'Adam, my darling,' Bianca began, just as shakily. 'I cannot hope to match those beautiful words. I am speechless with humility and wonder that you love me as you do. I ... I am not worthy of you ...'

Several people watching drew out handkerchiefs and there was much sniffling. Bianca's chin lifted and her eyes shone with love.

'But I will endeavour to be worthy,' she went on strongly. 'I promise always to love you. I promise always to be faithful to you. I promise never to let you down. You can count on me, my darling, just as I know I can always count on you.

'You gave me this beautiful gift today,' she said, fingering her pearls. 'But you gave me a greater gift the day you first gave me your friendship, then your undying love. Thank you, my husband.' And she reached up to kiss him.

The celebrant decided to abandon her prepared script. It just didn't seem to fit this touching moment. 'I wish to say I have never seen a couple so much in love,' she said, her eyes awash. 'And I am proud to pronounce them man and wife. May their lives be as long and as wonderful as their love for each other.'

Everyone stood up and clapped. It was much better than everyone crying. May lifted Tony up on the chair so that he could see better.

'Mum-Mum, Dad-Dad,' he said.

'Yes,' May murmured as she dashed away her own tears. 'And it's about time too.'

Did they honestly think they had fooled her all this time? She'd found out long ago they weren't really married, when she'd been staying at their unit that fortnight and picked up a photo album containing all those photographs of Adam's sister's wedding. She'd quickly guessed the reason for their deception and been very touched by it. But she was much better now. The doctors had given her a clean bill of health last month. The cancer was beaten.

Still, it wouldn't do to let on to Adam and Bianca that she knew the truth. They'd gone to so much trouble to keep deceiving her, with all their friends and Adam's relatives in on this special day. Besides, it wasn't as though she hadn't always been confident in their love and commitment to each other.

No, she would not tell them. Let them have their little secret. It didn't matter now that they were really married.

'Mum?' Bianca said, coming up to her with shining eyes and an adoring Adam on her arm. 'Before we get distracted with the party afterwards, we wanted to thank you again for minding Tony while we go on our second honeymoon.'

'My pleasure, darling. Tony and I will have such fun together, won't we?' She glanced up to find Tony had scrambled down from the chair and was running down towards his sandpit in the far corner of the garden, Lucky's little legs going hell for leather after him.

Bianca laughed. 'He'll make sure you sleep at night, that's for sure. Oh, and we have a little present for you which we hope you might like.'

'A present for me? But you don't have to reward me to mind my grandson!'

'No, it's not that kind of present.'

'Really? Now I'm intrigued. Well, what is it? Tell me.'

'There's going to be a little brother or sister for Tony some time in the New Year. Your guess is as good as mine when.'

May didn't know what to say. Her heart swelled to overflowing proportions and she hugged Bianca, looking at her proud son-in-law over her daughter's shoulder. 'Well done,' she told him, her eyes swimming. 'Oh, well done!'

P.S. It was a girl. And they called her May. Her arrival instantly turned her devil of a brother into an overly protective guardian angel. He insisted on sleeping in her room every afternoon, just in case

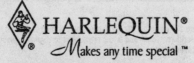

Take 2 bestselling love stories FREE

Plus get a FREE surprise gift!

Special Limited-Time Offer

Mail to Harlequin Reader Service®

3010 Walden Avenue
P.O. Box 1867
Buffalo, N.Y. 14240-1867

YES! Please send me 2 free Harlequin Presents® novels and my free surprise gift. Then send me 6 brand-new novels every month, which I will receive months before they appear in bookstores. Bill me at the low price of $3.12 each plus 25¢ delivery and applicable sales tax, if any*. That's the complete price, and a saving of over 10% off the cover prices—quite a bargain! I understand that accepting the books and gift places me under no obligation ever to buy any books. I can always return a shipment and cancel at any time. Even if I never buy another book from Harlequin, the 2 free books and the surprise gift are mine to keep forever.

106 HEN CH69

Name _____ (PLEASE PRINT) _____

Address _____ Apt. No. _____

City _____ State _____ Zip _____

This offer is limited to one order per household and not valid to present Harlequin Presents® subscribers. *Terms and prices are subject to change without notice. Sales tax applicable in N.Y.

UPRES-98

©1990 Harlequin Enterprises Limited

*The only way to be a bodyguard
is to stay as close as a lover...*

STAND BY ME

The relationship between bodyguard and client is always close...sometimes too close for comfort. This September, join in the adventure as three bodyguards, protecting three very distracting and desirable charges, struggle not to cross the line between business and pleasure.

STRONG ARMS OF THE LAW
by Dallas SCHULZE

NOT WITHOUT LOVE
by Roberta LEIGH

SOMETIMES A LADY
by Linda Randall WISDOM

*Sometimes danger makes
a strange bedfellow!*

**Available September 1998 wherever
Harlequin and Silhouette books are sold.**

Look us up on-line at: http://www.romance.net   PHBR998

MEN at WORK

All work and no play?
Not these men!

July 1998

MACKENZIE'S LADY by Dallas Schulze

Undercover agent Mackenzie Donahue's
lazy smile and deep blue eyes were his best
weapons. But after rescuing—and kissing!—
damsel in distress Holly Reynolds, how could
he betray her by spying on her brother?

August 1998

MISS LIZ'S PASSION by Sherryl Woods

Todd Lewis could put up a building with ease,
but quailed at the sight of a classroom! Still,
Liz Gentry, his son's teacher, was no battle-ax,
and soon Todd started planning some
extracurricular activities of his own....

MEN of STEEL

September 1998

A CLASSIC ENCOUNTER
by Emilie Richards

Doctor Chris Matthews was intelligent, sexy
and *very* good with his hands—which made
him all the more dangerous to single mom
Lizette St. Hilaire. So how long could she
resist Chris's special brand of TLC?

Available at your favorite retail outlet!

MEN AT WORK™

Catch more great

HARLEQUIN™ Movies

featured on **the movie channel** **tmc**

Premiering September 12th
A Change of Place
Starring Rick Springfield and
Stephanie Beacham. Based on the novel
by bestselling author Tracy Sinclair

Don't miss next month's movie!
Premiering October 10th
Loving Evangeline
Based on the novel by *New York Times*
bestselling author Linda Howard

If you are not currently a subscriber to
The Movie Channel, simply call your
local cable or satellite provider for more
details. Call today, and don't miss out
on the romance!

   **HARLEQUIN®**

100% pure movies.
100% pure fun.

*M*akes any time special ™

An Alliance Television Production

Don't miss these Harlequin favorites by some of our bestselling authors!